THE LOUSY ADULT

Johns Hopkins: Poetry and Fiction
*John T. Irwin, General Editor*

# The Lousy Adult

## Stories by William J. Cobb

Johns Hopkins University Press
*Baltimore*

This book has been brought to publication with the generous assistance of the G. Harry Pouder Fund and the Writing Seminars Publication Fund.

© 2013 Johns Hopkins University Press
All rights reserved. Published 2013
Printed in the United States of America on acid-free paper
9 8 7 6 5 4 3 2 1

Johns Hopkins University Press
2715 North Charles Street
Baltimore, Maryland 21218-4363
www.press.jhu.edu

Library of Congress Cataloging-in-Publication Data

Cobb, William J. (William James), 1957–
  [Short stories. Selections]
  The lousy adult : stories / by William J. Cobb.
    pages ; cm.
  ISBN-13: 978-1-4214-1147-7 (pbk. : acid-free paper)
  ISBN-10: 1-4214-1147-4 (pbk. : acid-free paper)
  ISBN-13: 978-1-4214-1148-4 (electronic)
  ISBN-10: 1-4214-1148-2 (electronic)
  I. Cobb, William J. (William James), 1957– Lousy adult. II. Title.
  PS3553.O199L68 2013
  813'.54—dc23      2013010208

A catalog record for this book is available from the British Library.

*Special discounts are available for bulk purchases of this book.*
*For more information, please contact Special Sales at 410-516-6936 or*
*specialsales@press.jhu.edu.*

Johns Hopkins University Press uses environmentally friendly book materials, including recycled text paper that is composed of at least 30 percent post-consumer waste, whenever possible.

*For Elizabeth & Lili*

I laid my fork carefully aside, and Jorge told his story. He was once living with his wife on an outpost in the jungle, washing gold and buying up the take of the other gold-washers. The family had at that time a native friend who brought his gold regularly and sold it for goods. One day this friend was killed in the jungle. Jorge tracked down the murderer and threatened to shoot him. Now the murderer was one of those who were suspected of selling shrunken human heads, and Jorge promised to spare his life if he handed over the head at once. The murderer at once produced the head of Jorge's friend, now as small as a man's fist. Jorge was quite upset when he saw his friend again, for he was quite unchanged except that he had become so very small. Much moved, he took the little head home to his wife. She fainted when she saw it, and Jorge had to hide his friend in a trunk. But it was so damp in the jungle that clusters of green mold formed on the head, so that Jorge had to take it out now and then and dry it in the sun. It hung very nicely by the hair on a clothesline, and Jorge's wife fainted every time she caught sight of it. But one day a mouse gnawed its way into the trunk and made a horrid mess of his friend. Jorge was much distressed and buried his friend with full ceremonies in a tiny little hole up on the airfield. For after all he was a human being, Jorge concluded.

"Nice dinner," I said to change the subject.

—from Thor Heyerdahl's *Kon-Tiki*

# CONTENTS

The Lousy Adult     1

The Sea Horse     29

Playboys     43

Warsaw, 1984     60

This Whatever We Have     78

The Next Worst Thing     102

What Happens to Rain?     121

That Night at the Café     136

Next Stop Palookaville     167

The Hidden Jesus     182

Acknowledgments     203

||||||||||||||||||||||||||||||||||||||||||||||||||||||||||||||||||||||||||||||||||||||||||||||||||||||||||||||||||||||

# The Lousy Adult

### DREAM JOB, WITH FINE PRINT

Joel Wind is gallery curator for the Taos Art Institute, and although he would have once considered this a dream job he hates it, actually. He loves art, but he's come to believe that most artists are at best troubled misfits and at worst vicious egotists. Based in New Mexico Joel is regularly required to nurse a gaggle of prima donna Southwestern poseurs, negotiating between their pet peeves and petty sensitivities as they strut about in paint-spattered cowboy boots spouting New Age hooey. Not to mention but we will the worrisome phone calls and E-mail. Plus he hates talking on the phone, that businessman voice he has to use. More than once he has hidden beneath his desk to avoid a drop-in visit. So he decides to hire an assistant.

He interviews five people for the job, five squirming encounters with the outside world, that uncontrollable realm that seems to throb and pulse with trouble, resentment, and desperation. The first two interviewees are sad, lumpy characters sent over from the state employment agency. Number one is a homely fellow with a long neck and enormous Adam's apple, as if he's swallowed a pet turtle. He vaguely recalls actually having been inside a museum but admits he does not do so on a regular basis, and confesses to being a bit fuzzy on the ins and outs of the biz. He asks if the Billy the Kid museum in Carson City counts. Joel says I don't see why not.

"It's not as fancy schmancy as this one, that's for sure. Like, there's no men's room inside the building, and if you gotta go, you end up in the nastiest portajohn in eastern New Mexico." He shivers and makes a face. "'Enough to gag a maggot, if you know what I mean."

Number two is a hepatitis-thin dirty brunette with long fingernails painted a dark, unusual shade of purple, which make her resemble a vampire's little sister. She confesses to possessing no typing skills but an eagerness to learn. Joel asks her what shade those nails are. They're unique. And he likes that, unique things.

"Root beer," she says. The look on her face is suspicious. "Is that a come-on?" she asks.

Joel assures her it is not.

The third is a pretty young man who likes art and seems promising. He's a witty one, he is, and Joel likes that. He's dressed smartly and makes a point of insisting that he never be referred to as a secretary. "I might be gay but I'm not menial," he says, which makes Joel laugh.

The fourth is so nervous it's a shame. Just looking at her, Joel feels as if he's on the *Titanic*, near the end, when the band's playing bravely and it's time to die. When Joel asks if she has any experience as an administrative assistant, her voice breaks when she replies, "I used to run postage stamp vending machines with my Mom, a year two ago."

The fifth is Ladonna Smith.

Ladonna is a short blonde in her thirties who admits she's been around the block a time or two but is it a sin to have led an adventurous life? She's been a PR person in Dallas, a folk singer in Phoenix, and a home improvement coordinator in Albuquerque. She has jiggly arms and heavy breasts and pronounced wrinkles in her neck. She wears turquoise and silver necklaces above her low-cut blouse, a brightly colored batik skirt, bracelets and bangles on her arms. From one of these dangles a kokopelli of a howling coyote she bought cheap off an authentic bruja in Las Cruces. Actually, she dabbles in watercolors herself. Joel admits that he also paints, oil mainly. He feels funny saying so, as if blurting out a secret love, something not to be confessed to strangers. Ladonna says she'd be thrilled to see them sometime. Joel shrugs, says it's nothing really. A personal thing.

"The best art is personal," says Ladonna. "Don't you think?"

At the end of the interview Joel smiles and says, "I think you're the one."

Before accepting the position, Ladonna has only one question: "Joel, do you believe in karma? You see, I think there are two kinds of people in the world. People who believe in karma and people who don't. The ones who believe know that everything you do—the good, the bad, and the ugly—comes back to you. They're the smart ones. They treat people right. They're not the kind who will fuck you over to get ahead. The ones who don't believe in karma aren't in touch with the cosmic scales. They deny them. They're the kind of people who will rent your cabin by the lake with a deposit check that ends up bouncing, litter the yard with beer cans and whiskey bottles, break a kitchen window, steal the mini-refrigerator, chop up the picnic table and the old sofa that's been in your family for years, for firewood, for a pagan bonfire, and leave repulsive stains on the sheets and toilet bowl. You know the kind."

Joel isn't sure that he does, but he'll take her word for it.

3

"So tell me," says Ladonna. Her voice is low and husky, like a bluesy lounge singer talking to the nightclub manager after too many cocktails and not enough applause. "You believe in karma?"

Joel blinks both eyes. His smile is two parts fear and one part ironic detachment. "That is not a question."

Ladonna nods and stares at his mouth. "That is not an answer."

Joel blinks both eyes again and hesitates. In the parking lot outside a car alarm begins wailing bloody murder. His stomach gurgles. Maybe this isn't a good idea after all. When is it officially too late to withdraw an offer of employment? Could he request a recount of the votes? Some of these ballots may have been improperly cast.

"I'd like to own a cabin by the lake," he says.

"What lake?"

"Any lake."

"No, you wouldn't. Well, sure. It's nice at first. Until the losers show up."

## Dream Life, with Inadequacy (see Fears of)

With Ladonna there to answer the phone and reply to E-mail Joel sets about the task of getting his life in order. He has come to the conclusion that he is not a good adult. Good adults are married with attractive wives or husbands who call if they are late coming home from the office or if they get held up in traffic. Good adults are coupled with spouses who care, who imagine horrible things are happening to them like being held at gunpoint in a tense hostage stand-off, the negotiators urging everyone "Jesus Christ! Just stay calm!" the overweight secretary sobbing, the bald no-nonsense real estate agent shouting, "You'll never get away with it!" the very pregnant woman with a long-suffering expression on her face meekly asking if she can please please go to the bathroom, please, it's urgent.

Joel is nothing like that.

He is not married. He has no children. If he's late anywhere no one will be worried or upset. His parents are both dead. He rarely speaks to his sister. The only person he really cares for, Beverly—who most people would call his girlfriend though Joel thinks the word somewhat ridiculous—lives in Seattle, over a thousand miles away.

If he died horribly in a bizarre accident, say, a fuel truck—one of those long aluminum things in which one can see one's reflection while driving behind it on the freeway, following too closely, perhaps—toppled off a freeway overpass at the exact moment he was walking beneath on his way to work and, say, he had forgotten his wallet (as he often does) and the truck exploded in a fiery inferno, traffic backed up for miles in both directions, the asphalt melted in black bubbles, and nothing was left of Joel but a charred, crushed corpse—not unlike those ancient Romans found covered in volcanic ash after the excavation of Pompeii—no one might realize it was him until they identified the body days or weeks later via dental records, via a crown he had put in place after breaking a tooth by accidentally biting down on a pebble misplaced God knows how or why in his turkey avocado sandwich.

No, he is not a good adult. Good adults have children and worry about them if they are sick, say, covered with red bumps is it a rash is it chicken pox is it measles oh Jesus tell me it's not the German measles! Let my baby live! Or if they're coughing hack hack hack are you all right, Sweetie? Is it diphtheria? Is it tuberculosis? Is it muscular dystrophy? Is it Creutzfeldt-Jakob disease? Oh please God don't take my baby! I promise I'll be good just don't take my baby!

Joel has no children, no wife. He and Beverly discussed marriage, once, but it was terribly abstract and theoretical, as if they were discussing adopting a Korean midget or learning to play the cello, something they would never do. They don't even know quite what to call each other—"girlfriend" and "boyfriend" seeming terms appropriate for teenagers wearing braces and being bored to death in the food court of the local mall, making lewd jokes about the corndogs.

Though it's true he has no offspring, now and then he entertains the notion of it—fatherhood, familydom. He and Beverly play a game known as What to Call the Baby. He thinks boys should be named after popular styles of socks or slacks: Argyle. Corduroy. Denim. Khaki. Crew. For her part, she thinks, for girls, fabrics will do nicely: Taffeta, Gaberdine, Satin, Madras, Lamé.

But good adults don't name their children oddly. Good adults pay for their child's piano and kabuki lessons, buy them scooters and video games as nonviolent as can be found but with all the Medieval gruesome pick-your-torture gizmos on the market it's not easy now is it.

## Dream House, with Semi-Attached Two-Car Anxiety Attack

Good adults own houses and swimming pools and cars and what does Joel own? Nothing. Nada. Zilch.

So he decides to buy a house. Though he is not a rich man, no Internet millionaire here, he has enough money. That's not the problem. It's just that the step is so big and he's not sure, really, whether he wants to stay in Taos the rest of his life. Buying a house, it's such a colossal step. So permanent, so irrevocable.

He knows that people buy and sell them all the time. He realizes that. He also knows he's not one of those people.

Still when he first considers buying a house, it seems like a marvelous idea. A man's home is his castle blah blah blah. A place to call your own. He mentions this thought, this whimsy, to friends and acquaintances.

They are full of advice.

Ladonna says he should watch out for carpeting. Stay away from it! It's full of mites. Tiny creatures you can't see that live off your skin, that feed off you while you're sleeping in your bed. Under a microscope, they resemble fierce if diminutive dragons. Hideous. Repulsive. And carpeting is chock full of them. That's where they breed. Mite orgies being a commonplace sight in the fibers of your average tapioca-colored shag carpeting, something you'd witness all the time if you could see things that small you're lucky you can't really believe me take my word for it.

Richard Kratch the New Age cowboy artist says, "Well you can't just buy a house, you know. You have to decide what style you want. That's an absolute must. So what's your poison?" he goads. "Santa Fe adobe? Split-level ranch? An A-frame? A postmodern dreamscape, all tubes and angles, like a Leger painting? Or maybe something with babyshit linoleum in the kitchen, a tacky fake chandelier over the dinette all tangled with an extension cord like horny snakes mating and an inflatable pool in the backyard into which your teen son masturbates à la Eric Fischl? Maybe a cluttered, Rauschenberg garage complete with a plastic terrarium in which a pet tarantula hunches nervously?"

They all say *Find a house that's right for you*. But what would that be? What kind of house fits a forty-four-year-old museum curator who cannot shake the feeling that he is incapable of managing his own life? Who fears he will live his allotted time and never experience true happiness? Who is obsessed with the idea that his head, hands, and feet are altogether too big—compared to the rest of his body, borderline gargantuan? Who feels like a middle-aged Pinocchio? Where do you find a fifteenth-century cobbler's hut in New Mexico?

So he ends up buying an adobe/stucco one-story that seems nice enough, rather nondescript and unremarkable, but the price is reasonable, though the mortgage payment pretty much eats up his paycheck and he better not lose his job, really, because there goes the house and most likely the great majority of the $69,836 he forked over in down payment plus closing costs, not to mention the six point five percent to a real estate agent who seemed to be doing a darn good underling-of-Satan impersonation.

## I'm the Person Your Mother Warned You About

In her first few months on the job, Ladonna charges ahead vigorously, reorganizing Joel's office, putting flowers on the reception desk and a new coffee pot—in which she heats water for herbal tea—in the office. Beside it nestles an assortment of Red Zinger, Orange Pekoe, and Darjeeling tins in a small wicker basket as if intended for a miniature picnic. She's constantly making tea and talking on the telephone, or at Joel's desk, using the computer. There is only one terminal and Joel has offered to share. He likes the flowers and when her constant voice on the telephone fills the office with mind-numbing noise, he can always leave.

His hours are flexible and Ladonna is only half-time. He likes the flowers. A woman's touch. Sometimes he sits on the longhorn-and-cowhide sofa while she's at the computer and simply gazes out the window. Outside there is a parking lot behind a row of pine trees, a series of adobe-style houses stretching toward the mountains in the distance, whose red earth and green trees could have been painted by Cezanne himself. When it seems as if Ladonna can shoulder the responsibility of the office, he sits back and daydreams of Navajo girls in a canyon stream, images of toasters and coffee makers floating Magritte-style beside puffy white clouds in the sky above . . . .

— — —

One Monday Ladonna walks into the office wearing upon her head what most closely resembles a cross between a cowboy hat and a box of valentine chocolates. She hangs it on the bent-willow coat rack and fluffs out her baby doll blonde locks. Over the weekend she's had her hair permed into a thick cluster of platinum blonde corkscrew curls. She asks Joel if he notices anything different.

He squints his eyes and feigns confusion. "I'm sorry. Have we met? In Hollywood, perhaps? At the starlet convention?"

Ladonna beams. "Oh, you," she says. "Stop."

But later in the week Ladonna's hands begin to loosen on the reigns of happiness. She arrives at nine and stays all day, complaining that the amount of work there is demands at least seventy hours a week, though she's only paid for twenty. He wants total commitment, doesn't he? Plus she needs a title that will command some respect. Associate Director would do nicely. She needs the other people in the organization to know she's not just a secretary. Like Ellen, the accountant. "I don't know what her problem is, honestly. She seems to think her shit don't stink."

Joel frowns. What's the matter with Ellen?

"Five minutes ago she said, 'Oh, Ladonna, you always dress so festive.' Which is code for what? Something bitchy, I'm sure. Like she's one to talk. Have you seen the bruises on her neck? If I wasn't so nice and hadn't been raised right I'd say, 'Ellen, aren't you a little O.L.D. for love bites?' But I keep my mouth shut. If she wants to make a spectacle of herself, more power to her. Though why the rest of us have to watch is beyond me."

Joel tells her he thinks she's overdoing it. Perhaps she should consider working less. "Don't knock yourself out," he says. "It isn't worth it." When she persists he grows impatient and adds, "That's all that's in the budget, okay? It's not up to me."

She leaves that afternoon, early. The next day, when she makes tea, she doesn't offer to make Joel any. Fine, he thinks. Be that way.

—  —  —

A few days later Ladonna demands to know why Joel has delayed the opening of Richard Kratch's one-man show, a retrospective of his desert pastels titled *The Gulch Manifesto*. Richard is a fifty-five-year-old ex-commune leader known for his metal sculptures of organ pipe cactus and lariats, not to mention an entire series of sandstone paintings of cowpokes and cattle rustlers against burnt orange sunsets, filigreed with a bit of Navajo geometrical hoopla on the borders, a nod to our Anasazi ancestors and their penchant for stick-figure petroglyphs. His hair is white, his face is ruddy, his eyebrows long, elaborate, and upsweeping, like the feathers of a cockatoo. When the wagon train of Robert Bly's *Iron John* wildman business headed out in the late eighties, Richard was one of the first aboard.

He and Ladonna have a thing going. Joel is not aware of this.

Ladonna says, "I don't know what your problem is, really. Richard's work is amazingly, awesomely brilliant."

Joel leans forward, puts his hands over his face, and slumps, surrendering to a kind of remains-of-the-day exhaustion. "Richard," he says, "is a worm. A total phony. A dolt."

"How can you say such a thing? He's so creative!"

Joel snorts. "He's got two ideas in his head and it's crowded."

"You're just jealous," says Ladonna.

"Are we talking about the same person? Richard Kratch? Bad cowboy artist?"

Ladonna frowns. "And sexy, too. Though I don't know why he puts up with Krysten."

Richard's wife, Krysten, is a famous gadabout at local shindigs, a painfully thin name-dropper who will be sweetness and light to the fatcats and Captain Bligh to the help.

"I heard they're into swapping," adds Ladonna.

Joel says he could have lived without that info, thank you very much. But more power to 'em. He's sure they'll give some pair of weirdoes a thoroughly gruesome run for their money.

"Oh, come on. You're not going to tell me you don't have the hots for Krysten?"

Joel rubs his face. "She's like some sixties housewife who used to be pretty before all the prescription drugs. Like Jackie-O on the tail end of a diet pill binge."

Ladonna frowns and sips her herbal tea. "Has anyone ever told you you are not the easiest person to communicate with?"

Joel turns his attention to the computer screen. Several moments later he says, "Dolphins communicate via clicks and whistles."

"Via? Who says via anymore?"

"I do."

"Want my advice?" asks Ladonna. "Lose it. Makes you sound bookish. Effete. Eggheadish."

"Thanks for the input."

"Prissy. Limpwrist. Supercilious."

Joel closes his desk drawer and locks it with a small key from the collection on his plastic Tony the Tiger keychain. He pulls on his sport coat and picks up his leather satchel. "I'm leaving now. Via the door."

## Good Girls Go to Heaven, Bad Girls Go Everywhere

Ladonna soon mushrooms into a Major Problem. The office seems to contract into a smaller and smaller space, pushing Joel closer and closer to this person he begins to find repulsive. Her physical presence is overwhelming, overpowering, smothering. The odor of her body fills the very air that Joel must breathe. The smell of her begins to become a part of the office, a fog of her misty molecules and corpuscles. Joel can feel it filling his lungs.

And Ladonna is seriously funky. She eats too much garlic. How do you tell a person she stinks? You don't. Joel's not about to.

Plus her voice is too loud. In normal conversations she seems to be almost shouting. She remembers things in her own way, in her own world, and she can amplify every slight in her mind into a serious personal insult and slam of her fragile ego and dubious character.

One day when she is complaining about how hard she's working and how the money isn't worth it, that really, she can probably make more money waiting tables at La Palm D'Or, where her sister works and makes two hundred dollars a night in tips alone, easy, and Joel is ready to tell her Well do it then and get off my back, what he actually says is, "Okay, Ladonna. Okay." He pushes down with both hands in the air, like a conductor suggesting diminuendo.

She goes on and on about how they should really be doing something special to promote Richard's show. "I know you're the boss and everything, and the boss is always right, but Richard is internationally famous, right? Am I right or am I right? And can we afford a lousy four-color brochure? No. Why not? Tell me. Why not?"

Joel puts his hands over his ears. "I'm right here," he says. "You don't need to shout."

"Who's shouting? I'm not shouting."

"Well let's not get all worked up about—"

"You're the one who's getting worked up. Listen to you. You're the one who's shouting."

"Ladonna—"

She tells him she just needs to vent.

"This is a professional office," says Joel. "You need to vent, go out in a field somewhere. Not here."

For a moment, as she glares at him, the room sizzles with furious bands of electrical, emotional discharge. Joel does his best to ignore Ladonna and she closes her eyes, breathes deeply for ten seconds, then says, "Oh, forget it." She stands up and stalks to the coat rack, where she pulls on her ridiculous red woolen cloak, the one that makes her resemble nothing so much as a plump, middle-aged Little Red Riding Hood. She flashes Joel a smile full of fierce bitterness that hints for years people have been doing this to her and now you too, so this is the way it's going to be?

"Ladonna . . . ."

Before slamming the door, she hisses, "I wasn't shouting. And I don't like being spoken to in that condescending tone of voice. You don't pay me enough to put up with this crap, thank you very much, so I'll be looking for other work immediately. I've had other offers. Good-bye!"

Joel accepts that as her two-week notice and, before he leaves the office that day, posts the job opening on the arts commission list serve. He figures it will all be for the best. Ladonna will get a new job and he'll get a new assistant and everyone will be happy. Right?

## It's Been Lovely but I Have to Scream Now

Storming away from the office Ladonna is internally screaming all the lines she'd had the good sense not to shout in the office because goddamnit she's a professional. Lines like *Thank you for ruining my life, you tightwad bastard! I could do a better job in my sleep, you dickless wonder! Have a shitty life, asshole!*

Another part of her is whimpering. Why does she always get the short end of the stick? Would it be so difficult for things to go her way just for once? Would that be so difficult? All she wants is to have a party, a celebration for Richard, whose exhibit is coming out, is making a big splash, is on the lips of everyone who is anyone, is the thing they are all talking about. In fact she promised Richard she would do whatever she could. She's only trying to help, only trying to lend a hand.

She drives to the supermarket like a teenage kid who's just barely passed Driver's Ed and wants to establish a sense of empowerment by speeding through school zones. No matter what they say, she is not duplicitous, vengeful, and scheming. She can kill them with kindness when she has to and she will by god she will. She's misunderstood is what she is. Passionate. Like Marilyn Monroe, whom she resembles. The same peroxide blonde hair, the same voluptuous figure. (Only much shorter.)

Plus she has just changed her antidepressant prescription and that is definitely part of the tangle. It makes her mouth dry and kills her sex drive, but that's just as well, since something had also given her a rash on the inside of her elbows and her thighs and that is definitely not a turn-on. From her elbows to her knees, a mess of pink bumps, ugh. She wears a long-sleeved deep purple madras muumuu-type dress to cover it up, and to allow her body a dynamic, flowing quality. Still, the constant itching is not a good thing. And there sits Joel, in his sweet office at the Arts Commission, keyboarding E-mail at the computer and looking unshakable in a crisp white shirt, jeans, and moccasins. His skin is clear, his eyes deep green, the tips of his ears an elfish pink. The healthy bastard.

The way Ladonna sees it, Joel thinks he's better than everyone else. He doesn't go out much in town, is never seen drinking and carousing with the other artists like Lionel and Barry Gench, who think him a sissy (and, most likely, queer) for his holier-than-thou ways. Joel pretends not to care. He makes out like he's had his wild days and his embarrassing moments. Once he even told Ladonna,

"I've wasted plenty of time being fucked up, but I don't regret a day that I've been sober."

Now he claims to like his privacy. He says he likes to be on his own. Not to have people poking their noses in his business. But Ladonna knows it's all an act. He's up to something. Or, as her mother liked to put it, up to no good.

## A Pleasant New Home, with Psycho Lurking in Yard

Joel's new house is a boxy thing with windows round as portholes. It's a dirty white color, the shade of old doilies or the wedding veils left over from bad, broken marriages. The backyard is thick with fallen leaves brown as ripped pieces of cardboard, enclosed by a sagging gray chain link fence, against which some of the leaves are pinned. It's early evening. In the east, just above the alley that borders the back fence, hangs a sliver of yellow moon. The air smells of dead apples and is so cold the sound of the leaves beneath Ladonna's shoes seems unnaturally loud.

She crouches beside the pine and struggles to work the dull end of a sharpened stick into the pile of leaves directly in front of the back gate. Her breath puffs in clouds of white frost and her hair hangs in her face. She knows she's doing the right thing. This bastard thinks he can get away with treating her like shit like some old Medieval hag well he's got another thing coming. The pointed end of the stick protrudes a few inches out of the ground, but she covers it with leaves. It is invisible. Next time Joel goes to take out his trash, he's in for a surprise.

She crouches against a pine tree on the hill behind Joel's backyard and watches his living room with binoculars. The woods are swarming with bugs, beetles and ants and spiders and woolly worms and who knows what. She has the persistent feeling there are cobwebs in her face.

Inside his living room, Joel sits on the sofa, wondering whether he should get up and call the vet. His dog, Whistle, is shivering uncontrollably and panting too hard. They just returned from a long walk in the woods and Whistle has overdone it. She chased a rabbit up a hill, whimpering as she ran. She seemed to be whimpering because she knew she'd never catch the rabbit. Now she's exhausted and trembling. It's as if she has hypothermia but isn't cold. Joel scratches her forehead and frowns. Whistle is one of the few things he loves in the world and he's afraid he's killed her by walking her too far. But she loves to walk. To run. Whenever Joel picks up his car keys or laces up his boots or gets out her leash, she'll jump and whimper, her ears perked up, tail wagging.

In the yard outside, Ladonna leans against the pine to attempt to still the jittering of her binoculars. Observing his life through these windows is murder. The colors of the image in the binoculars blur together, and she cannot stop them from jiggling. It's as if she were watching a constellation through a cheap telescope. After kneeling on one leg and leaning against the tree so long her knee goes numb, she struggles to straighten up. Brushing cobwebs and pine needles off her shoulder, she flicks her hand against a sticky patch on her shoulder and finds she has been leaning against thick dribbles of pine sap. Oh god. Her elbows are itching and her shoulders are sticky and just what is Joel doing with that dog? Trying to back away, she steps on a rake, jerking the handle forward and banging herself in the head. The pain is hot and hard, taking her breath for a moment. To recover she bends over double, squealing for a moment and panting.

Whistle catches the noise and begins barking. Holding her by the leash, Joel opens the back door and flips on the outside lights. Panicking, Ladonna rushes toward her car parked on the street behind Joel's house, bashing her head against the low-lying branches of a juniper.

In the October sky hangs the hunter's moon. The middle of Joel's back itches, the sensation not unlike that of someone upon which a cruel wag has pinned a bullseye target scrawled with the legend "Shoot me!"

### You Used Me and I Thank You for It

When Ladonna reaches home she's covered with scratches, juniper and pine needles stuck against the pine sap on her clothes and in her hair, a dark bruise on her cheek. Her husband, Mitch, isn't home. He's attending a black-and-white photography course and has converted part of the basement into a dark room. His favorite subject is abandoned farms and mills and gas stations with weeds growing up through the pavement and cracks in the concrete. Weeds are a common thread in his photos. Ladonna's sister Paula is there instead, coming over to do laundry because her washing machine is on the fritz. Ladonna finds her in the den, folding a blue bath towel and smoking a cigarette, holding it in her mouth as she make a crease in the towel pinned against her waist.

"Well guess what the cat drug in," says Paula, squinting through a film of smoke.

One of Paula's boyfriends, the sarcastic one whose name Ladonna can never remember, Mick or Vick or Rick, something that rhymes with *ick*, sits in the living room staring at a copy of *Money* magazine. "I need to bone up on investment strategy," he'd told Paula when he sat down. He has more credit card debt than three years of income as a bartender and the most substantial thing he owns is a jet-ski with clogged intake valves his brother let him borrow and still leaves angry threatening messages on his answering machine demanding When are you going to return my fucking jet-ski!

When Paula first sees Ladonna she treats the moment as a joke, because everything she says around this boyfriend tends to be sarcastic and jokey. Around him, she also drinks and smokes. Paula is a chameleon girlfriend, acting different around her different boyfriends. At the moment Ladonna can number three. One is sporty, the hang-glider/parachutist/bungie jumper chap. The other is an advertising dude who writes "language poetry," whatever that is. The sarcastic one is a putative artist, at least he refers to himself as such, but when Ladonna learned he collects "found" art, she said, "That doesn't really count, does it?" Paula just shrugged, saying, "You got me. Far as I can tell it's just a flea market without the tent."

Paula's boyfriends are never particularly legit, but she's good looking and there are always more where those came from. She flirts with Mitch too much, no doubt envying Ladonna's serenity and security. At least Ladonna imagines so. When once asked why she wasn't married, Paula replied, "Because you're doing such a knock-down job of it." And Ladonna couldn't quite tell if she was mocking or sincere.

On the night of Ladonna's return from the botched spying at Joel's new pad, after noticing the odd look on her face, Paula changes her tone and asks softly, "What happened to you?"

"Joel did this," says Ladonna. "He attacked me in the park."

— — —

Paula gets her a glass of wine and wet washcloth. Ladonna sits in the kitchen, her hands shaking, squeezing a wad of paper towels in her hands. She says that Joel hit her and threatened to make her pay if she didn't keep her mouth shut about this and he swore he'd kill her he really would and she believes it that man is capable of anything.

"Did he hit you with his fist?" asks Rick.

Ladonna says she doesn't know. She thinks he slapped her. It all happened so fast.

"So you're telling us your boss slugged you?" asks Rick, his voice tinged with amusement. "Hasn't he ever heard the old 'Help is hard to find'?"

Ladonna and Paula stare at him.

Rick shrugs and waves them off, like what a pair of buzzcrushers.

"Asshole," says Paula. She takes Ladonna by the arm and pulls her toward the back bedroom.

As they move away, Rick calls out, "I was just kidding!"

Paula shuts the bedroom door. She asks Ladonna what started all this, where they were, what she could remember. Ladonna insists it's all too hazy, like she's trying to look at it and can't see it clearly, you know? "It's like I'm trying to block it out. Everything's foggy and hazy. When I try to remember it all, it's like I'm watching it on TV. Only the picture is all fuzzy and out of focus."

Paula insists it shouldn't be that hard to remember. "It's not like ancient history. This just happened, right?"

"I think so." Ladonna's eyes are red and puffy and full of tears. "My face hurts."

"Think so? You're not positive? Did someone else hit you? You're sure it was Joel?"

"I don't know. It was dark."

What was she doing in the park at night? She had no idea. Was that Kit Carson or Baca Park? She doesn't know that, either. And no, she doesn't want to call the police. She doesn't want anyone asking a bunch of questions. She's tough. She can handle this.

"What park are you talking about?" Paula repeats.

"If you're going to use that tone of voice, I just won't tell you."

"Ladonna . . . ."

"Look at you. My own sister playing blame-the-victim."

Paula says that isn't it at all and Ladonna knows it. She says, "Something funny is going on here, isn't it? Fess up, Don. What is it?"

Paula can smell the fishiness of this story from a mile away. She tells Ladonna that really, it just doesn't make sense, is all. She shouldn't go starting something ugly. "It's wrong, is what it is."

## It's as Bad as You Think and They Are Out to Get You

Ladonna arrives at work wearing what Joel presumes to be some kind of period costume or traditional apparel for aboriginal cultures in Burkina Faso or deepest darkest outer New Guinea. The dress is a slinky material the electric green color of key lime pies. It's decorated with a batik pattern of lipstick red pelicans swallowing baby blue crocodiles. Ladonna declares that she wants to have a word with him. Her face is bruised and puffy. Her hands are sweating and as she stands before Joel in the small office, she unfolds a sheet of paper upon which is typed her list of reasons for instigating a sexual harassment law suit against her former employer, specifically Joel Martin Wind, for mental and physical abuse presently causing her intense anxiety, emotional turmoil, and spiritual malaise. As she reads aloud from the list, Joel watches her hands, how they tremble, how their dampness creates smudges on the paper.

By the time she's finished he has his head in his hands. The only thing he can think of to say is, "Why are you doing this to me?"

"Number one," she says, "you are not an adult. You are an immature and vain and shallow person. Witness how you cannot make even the simplest of decisions, such as where to go for lunch or which artist to promote. You are an adolescent and like most if not all the men in this country suffer from an arrested development exemplified by but not limited to perpetual puberty. I would not be surprised if you kept *Playboy* magazines beneath your mattress."

"Number two: This is not what I need to be doing at this particular moment in time. It is crucial to make the right choices in life and I HAVE MADE THE WRONG CHOICE. YOU ARE A BAD PERSON." She pauses long enough to offer him a smile intended to burn a hole through that undersized, underused, hopefully soon-to-be-clogged-with-cholesterol-deposits lump of muscle he calls a heart. "For lack of more forceful expressions, I hate you. Pond scum would have to undergo millions of years of evolution to reach a level lower than you—"

"Ladonna. . . . Maybe this is not—"

"Not the appropriate topic of discussion for your office? Not professional?"

"Well what I was going to say was—"

"Save it for your next victim, Vlad. I'm not through with you yet. There are two kinds of people in the world. People who use people and people who get used. You are the former. I am the latter. But not anymore, Buster! Not anymore!"

With that she grabs the plastic model of a giant squid Joel keeps on his computer top and throws it out the window, shouting is that what he thinks she is, a toy, is that it? That he can throw away whenever he wants to? Well how does he like it when she throws out his toys, Mr. Maturity? Mr. Professional? Huh? Huh?

She leaves with an explosive slam. In the aftermath of her frenzy, Joel's ears ring maddeningly. He notes to himself that actually there are three kinds of people in the world. People who believe there are two kinds, people who don't, and people who fit into no category whatsoever, whose behavior and motivation is so directionless and unpredictable that if all the psychiatrists in the world put their heads together they could only scratch.

## Never Underestimate the Power of Stupid People in Large Groups

After threatening to see her lawyer pronto and make his life one miserable fucking court proceeding, Ladonna second-thoughts it a bit. She even does her best to keep her mouth shut. She tells Mitch she tripped in the backyard on the garden hose and he promises, next time, to coil it. But Paula's sarcastic boyfriend, Rick, tells Raymond Hosselkus that Mr. Faggy Museum Dude Joel had either slapped Ladonna around or that the wacky chick had made the whole thing up and Hosselkus—whom everyone called Hoss and who liked a good story when he heard one—told Edie Carlyle and she told Jolanda Ramirez and somehow Ed Malcolm, Jack Trest, Gracie Benavidez, and the Carbo sisters found out about it. Being an old friend of Ladonna's husband, Mitch, Jack Trest volunteered to kick Joel's ass for him, and that's how Mitch heard the story, since Jack thought Mitch already knew all about it and simply wasn't doing anything because he didn't want to get charged with assault. It takes less than a week from the time Rick says something to when Mitch finds out. By the time Mitch hears the story, Joel is accused of slapping her repeatedly, ripping her dress, and trying "to do something nasty to her," though he is supposed to have given up when a softball team arrived at the park.

— — —

It also happens that Mitch has a brother by the name of Deuce who is known as one badass cop—the angry, veteran patrolmen type, the been-making-too-little-money-for-too-long type. Deuce is the fifteenth or sixteenth person—by that point the actual sequence of who blabbed what to whom in what order had become rather tangled—to hear that Joel had "bitch-slapped" Ladonna. Even though Mitch tells him Ladonna refuses to press charges "because she wants to put this behind her" Deuce offers to fix Joel's wagon but good. To put the hurt on him. To do what needed to be done. To set things right in the world. A thing like that can't go unpunished, can it? Maybe a broken finger or two. Fuck, maybe a broken hand. An arm. It could be done. Legally. There were loopholes. Being at least one digit, one pinky, on the long arm of the law, he knows some things. "Let me catch that fucker going so much as one mile over the line. So much as a right tail light out, and he'll be getting friendly with some new pals in county jail."

Ladonna's brother-in-law the Angry Cop looses an ugly grin. "He'll learn *regret*, the sonofabitch."

## The Light at the End of the Tunnel Is an Oncoming Train

At this point in his life Joel believes that he doesn't ask much from the outside world. He only wants to be left alone. He wants peace. He loves his art and he loves his nothing-special new house and sometimes he fools himself into feeling like he'll stay in Taos forever if the phone doesn't ring too much and he'll be almost happy. He loves his dog, Whistle, and he loves a good woman, Beverly, though she lives so far away and he sees her so seldom that she sometimes seems a mirage created to make him appear less solitary and unwanted.

What most people don't realize, what Joel only senses now and then, is that not only is he an artist but he's nothing less than The Real Thing. He cringes at the thought. He doubts himself, doesn't have the confidence of others, and doesn't want to imitate the Loud and Obnoxious he sees barking all around him. Self-effacing to a fault, he thinks of his work as an odd hobby, like composing chess problems or blowing glass figurines of penguins and walruses. He paints large canvases that appear in galleries now and then, to mixed reviews. Some people rave and some people shrug. At age forty-four he doesn't expect to have the crown of fame dropped on his head any time soon.

He makes a living as a curator and that's something.

When he first notices odd stares and glances in the supermarket and restaurants he frequents, he tries to ignore them. He tells himself paranoia is for chumps. Then Lana Goodnight E-mails Beverly the scuttlebutt. Beverly calls to warn him the same day Deuce's deputy sheriff buddy gives him a ticket for nothing. When Joel complains that he's innocent, the beefy imitation Barney Fife jabs him in the gut with a nightstick, slams his face against the cruiser's hood, and books him for resisting arrest.

In the slammer, Joel lies on a dank, mildewy mattress in a wretched, dirty metal cage. There is a toilet on one side of the cell, bunk beds on the other, a wall of bars looking out at a hallway, across from more cells, more bars, all painted a horrific shade of orange. There is idiotic profanity scrawled on the walls, cut into it with knives. His cellmate is a skinny Mexican-American kid named Carlos who's accused of selling dope. He says it's all bullshit, honest. Sure, he gets high now and then, but that reefer wasn't his, the whole thing was a setup.

Joel believes him.

The next day Beverly flies into town and bails him out.

"Baby, baby," she says, stroking his head as he hugs her and tries not to sob. "What in the world have you gotten yourself into?"

While he's out on bail, Wanda Shumaker, chairperson of the board of trustees of the arts commission, asks for his resignation. She insists she didn't believe it at first but where there's smoke there's fire. There was a board meeting the night before, and a decision was made. Of course they heard all about how Joel slugged that cop and tried to take his gun away as he was being arrested on suspicion of sexual assault and battery. At the meeting Wanda tried to stand up for him, she did. "Why would Joel do such a thing?" She implored the other trustees to consider that they might not know the whole story. "He's always been such a gentle person."

King Peterson, the one trustee who had never liked Joel, told her he had inside dope that truth be told, this was just the tip of the iceberg. "I heard he was jonesing for some blow," said King. "The tail end of a coke binge takes no prisoners." He had never done drugs in his life but he knew the lingo. "Cokeheads turn pretty nasty when the snow runs out."

— — —

While Joel is in jail two high school kids who live across from him, Bart and Brad Thompson, spray-paint CHILD MOLESTERS DIE! on his garage door. They tell their friends that sick fuck better watch his ass or he's going to get a pipe bomb enema, yeah!

After a few weeks of this Joel is thoroughly freaked out. All he wants is to be left alone and every day there seem to be new people who hate him, new swarthy villagers who clatter and rattle outside the castle walls, gesticulating with their pitchforks, waving their smoky torches, gossip-dialing their cell phones, their ghastly faces half death masks and half idiotic country-western singer grins.

Privately he calls Ladonna a psychobitch but knows that doesn't help anything. He retains a lawyer and from what he hears, his chances range from dramatic trial antic to desperate plea bargain.

Beverly sees the courtroom as a lose-lose proposition. She thinks there's only one way out of this hell. "Talk to her. Talk to this Ladonna person. If you have to, grovel."

## ALWAYS REMEMBER YOU'RE UNIQUE, JUST LIKE EVERYONE ELSE

On the day of their tête-à-tête, Joel feels the queasy stomach and sweaty palms of stage fright, as if he's about to play the violin at

Carnegie Hall and hasn't practiced in months. They've agreed to meet at a trendy coffee shop in a popular location off the main drag in Taos. Though it's not far, Joel must squint his eyes and concentrate with unholy fervor to keep from running onto the sidewalk and killing several pedestrians.

That morning it's raining gustily. The wind whips splatters from gutter spouts and eaves onto the sidewalks. A wet dog is leashed to the parking meter into which Joel feeds two quarters. Untangling it from the base of the meter Joel says, "Hey there, Pup. Try not to get wet."

Inside The Aisle of Java, Joel takes one of the booths along the front windows, composing himself at a wooden table with a lacquered top in which are placed newspaper advertisements from the 1890s—miracle pills, sewing machines, bicycles, and bonnets. Joel orders a double latte and for all the eye contact he makes in the room would not have reacted had Julia Roberts been sitting across from him. The unprocessed sugar is packaged in brown packets and, tearing it clumsily, Joel scatters the sandy, sticky grains across the illustration of a pince-nez.

As he brushes crumbs off the tabletop, which smells faintly of ammonia cleanser, the electrically charged figure of his former administrative assistant squeezes through a narrow space between two nearby tables and, as he wipes the sugar and ammonia off his hands, is upon him. Ladonna wears a voluminous deep purple muumuu caftan thing and appears to have gained weight. Her hands are pudgy and spotted with freckles, while her face is powdered eerily white, contrasting sharply with the black arcs of her brows and the peroxide blonde curls of her latest washed-up Vargas girl do.

She says hello like an estranged wife at a divorce-action deposition. While realizing it makes no sense, Joel witnesses himself asking, How are you?

In point of fact, she's fine. No. She's better than that. She's terrific. The Fourth National Bank of Casper, Wyoming, has recently bought one of her watercolors. The one with the ducks and dead trees against a gaunt sky, remember? Like a cross between Georgia O'Keefe and Andrew Wyeth? You liked it, or at least you said you did. Yes, everything is peachy. She's a winner. A fighter. A survivor. Let me repeat: a winner. You see, she always wins because she has to win she has to come out on top she has to defeat she has to be better than everyone else even though there are people who don't believe this who want to squash her choke her hold her down remind her constantly that THEY ARE SUPERIOR AND SHE IS INFERIOR that she's not exactly one of the chosen point out exactly where she fails just this or that disgusts me where here or there you miss the mark how she's not pretty enough how she's not smart enough how perhaps she could stand to lose some weight perhaps she's a bit emotional at times but she is not crazy she is not emotionally unbalanced she is not a menace to society is not a pathetic loser no matter how many people want her to be no matter how many times she's lost god knows it's too much to count it's not fair goddamnit it's not fair.

"That's why I wanted to see you, I think," said Joel. "I mean, I don't have anything against you, Ladonna. I know you're mad at me and that somehow I hurt you and I'm sorry for it, really I am. I mean, I know, I know you feel I've harmed you and if I did, I'm sorry. Really."

For a moment Ladonna merely stares in Joel's direction, giving his face the barest of lingering recognitions. In that moment, she seems to deflate. She sips her coffee and raves about the Sumatran blend they have there. The best beans outside of Santa Fe. And if he likes a fabulously rich taste he should try their French roast. Not for the faint-hearted, that's for sure.

"Apology accepted," she adds. "I don't hold a grudge. No one can ever say Ladonna Smith doesn't know how to forgive." But she wants to make one thing clear: She has not been talking behind his back. If other people want to shoot off their yaps, that's their business. She is not a backstabber. She wants to make that clear.

As she continues to talk, her mixture of entreaties and denials confuses Joel until he struggles to keep a visage of repulsion off the brittle, crinkled contours of his forced, I'm-glad-we-got-this-over-with smile. Across the street the adobe storefronts shimmer a sandy orange and his consciousness floats toward that haze, thinking, Who are these people in the world? Why do they do what they do?

# The Sea Horse

Because the Murdos lived in 17 for over eight months now and that was so long in the transient world of The Sea Horse that they had become part of the atmosphere, like the drunken seadog fog that drifted in autumn nights from the bay across Pelican Avenue or the blue devil mosquitoes that whined and stung and tormented one and all by the pool late summer evenings. Sloop found himself behind the Murdos' bathroom window, standing in the bamboo thicket. Through the glass he watched the woman turn on the shower and pull her dark hair back in a ponytail. The vanity-mirror light cast an aquamarine glow in the small bathroom as if she were a black velvet angelfish in an aquarium. She pulled her dress over her head. Sloop held his breath. He did not slap the mosquitoes biting his arms and neck.

The skin of her breasts and bikini strap lines glowed blacklight-white against the rest of her tanned flesh, her nipples cinnamon and small and forbidden. She scratched her neck and looked at herself in the mirror, the water hissing in the shower, a faint steamy mist drifting above the pole holding the shower curtain. She blew her nose. She stepped out of her striped panties and turned her back to Sloop. Her hips were wide and tan-lined, her cheeks round and dimpled pale in the greenish glow, cleft and curved like a pair of half-moons in twinned eclipse. While disappearing behind the goldfish-patterned shower curtain, she glanced in the direction of the window, of Sloop, her expression one of carefulness, of calmness, of a queer and curious relief.

—  —  —

Because the first two weeks he worked there Sloop didn't hear her say a word until one day he was cutting grass behind their room and she came out to ask if he'd like maybe a lemonade or something. Her face looked a little off. It wasn't until he saw her up close and personal that he noticed violet blotches on her cheeks and forehead. Her lips, puffy and cracked. Most days she wore a pair of huge dark oblong sunglasses that resembled the eyes of insects. She'd sit by the pool, her face resembling a giant wasp, smoking cigarettes and sipping cans of Diet Coke. If a car pulled into the driveway suddenly, she'd flinch.

Because her husband, George Murdo, drove a fabulous car. It was a 1957 Chevrolet Bel Air. A wide and stylish two-door convertible, it had a curved bulbous windshield big as a truck's, low sleek fins on the fenders like a Martian space-mobile, and a coyote skull hanging from the rearview. Its body was painted a fabulous deep-sea green, the color of bottle glass licked by mermaids with bright pink tongues.

Sloop admired the car and frowned whenever he saw its rightful owner, who boasted he'd won it playing stud poker, walking toward it, dangling his keys at the ready.

—  —  —

Because behind the motel, behind the gray wooden slatted fence that encompassed the wild bamboo thicket clusters of banana trees and overgrown sward of St. Augustine grass that elbowed oppressively hot and mosquito-filled around the guest room patios, stood an abandoned convenience store gently rusting and rotting in the tropical heat and sun. The asphalt of the parking lot was cracked and full of weeds, littered with broken beer bottles. The windows were scrawled spray-painted ugly with graffiti, swastikas, elaborate leering wolf faces, and the romantic skills of a one Camille Ladoux. On the roof, the air was sea-soaked and balmy. In late afternoon it glowed with a tangerine light as the sun filtered through the rustling palms. In early evening the sky turned violet, the world filled with a smell of beached catfish, cut grass, and tar.

Because from there Sloop watched the Murdos' bedroom and bathroom windows without fear of discovery, necessary in the hours after George had returned home from wherever he went each day.

Because from there he saw George Murdo slap his wife. It unfolded in dumb show, the sound of hand on cheek muted completely by the distance and magnified only as a vibration by binoculars pressed against Sloop's eyes, blurred by his eyelashes, the entire squalid scene experienced as if watching a silent film of humiliation and disgrace.

Because to Sloop it seemed as if he were witnessing the slow domination of the world by horrid soldiers in the pod people brigade.

— — —

Because Sloop's father and mother were no longer alive and present. Because he wasn't and she wasn't and they weren't and never would be again. That was part of the problem. Sloop blamed their absence on the pod people but ultimately it was the handiwork of D.J. Bowles.

Sloop's father had been Band Director at Cameron County Consolidated High School. D.J. played the tuba. He was a skinny, scrawny kid who threw lighted kitchen matches on the weaker students and yanked the girls' skirts whenever Mr. Reed, Sloop's father, had his back turned. When reprimanded, D.J. stood in sullen and pimple-faced silence, smirking if asked a simple question like, "How would you feel if someone burned your neck?"

Sloop overheard his parents discussing D.J. at breakfast, and late at night. What he remembered later was his father saying, "I don't know about kids like that. He's one of the pod people, I guess. Like in that Body Snatchers movie. They look and sound like human beings but they don't have an ounce of goodness in them. Just meanness and spite and smartassedness. And I don't know what to do about it. I really don't."

What he did was expel D.J. after he shamed Alice Lankewish so badly she couldn't talk. Lionel Evans, a large boy with fleshy extrusive gray warts on his neck, was a better tuba player anyway. A month later D.J. met Sloop's father in the parking lot behind the field where the band practiced. Mr. Reed had opened the passenger side door and was climbing in when D.J. walked up, saying, "Hey, Mr. Reed, hold up." Sloop's father turned to look and D.J. raised a shotgun and blew his face off. Then he leaned in and blasted Sloop's screaming mother. Everyone watched as he walked back to his car, tossed the gun in, and drove away, tires smoking as he laid rubber, loosing a rebel yell.

Now he was in prison and said he was Sorry. He claimed he was driven to it via a combination of pornography, methamphetamines, and martial arts video games. He said he never meant to hurt anybody. He didn't know what got into him.

— — —

Because the motel was eggshell stucco beside a green and sluggish sea and was so cheap when people checked in and signed the old-fashioned register it was like a release form for no complaints. They arrived at the last minute, needing a place for the night, and left early the next morning, trying to avoid contact with the others, the weeklies and monthlies who somehow liked the fleabag atmosphere and rank and lovely abandon. Its claim to stylishness was the fanciful figure of its sign, The Sea Horse, the matching icon with its curving stallion neon amber neck and spiny neon emerald mane. Plus the loopy letters of the neon grapefruit script in the office window usually read Vacancy.

When Sloop got a job there afternoons in mid-summer his cousins laughed and laughed and declared him to be some kind of Guinness World Record Loser for stooping so low.

"I mean, Jesus," they said. "Can't you do any better? We'll be embarrassed for people to hear of this."

"Shut up," he said. "They pay real money. Plus no one bothers me. I like that."

Sloop's skin was pink and his hair spiky short and white as an albino shoe brush. He was always sunburned, his nose peeling to reveal a more tender, painful shade of pink, the skin flaking off in splotches, and a faint fuzz of white hair covering his pink slightly too large ears. Birth name David, when his parents were alive he was always known as Sloopy. Now his cousins nicknamed him Strawberry. They had great fun with this moniker though he didn't like being known as a fruit. He pretended not to care but his cousin Jim who thought he was God's gift to high school cheerleaders suffered two weeks of intense agony itching and whining after Sloop rubbed poison ivy in his clean jockey briefs, placed them back in his dresser drawer natural as pie, and walked around the house all through the scabby ordeal doing his best to hide a pawky grin.

— — —

Because at The Sea Horse, he never knew who he might see. Legend had it that Rita Hayworth once stayed there, on a wild ride from Hollywood to New Orleans. Mr. Buzzy, the lush manager, insisted it was the Lord's truth.

Sloop asked Who's Rita Hayworth?

Mr. Buzzy said Oh nobody really. Just the most beautiful movie star that ever was.

— — —

Because the seeing of things was also part of the problem.

Sloop feared the pod people, and he feared going mentally blind. It bothered him that if he closed his eyes and tried to picture all the people he knew—girls at school, his cousins, his Aunt Darna, and most importantly, his parents—he couldn't do it. No image came to mind. This made him doubt himself. His faculties. It made him wonder if he was secretly somehow a Retard.

After spying on the woman in 17, though, his mental vision bloomed. He saw her quite clearly. Her pale breasts, uncovered, the nipples circular and stiff and golden, her lovely collar bones, her neck in shadow, a tattoo of vines encircling her left arm, her black oak ponytail, her thin face covered with dark bangs like a horse's forelock.

— — —

Because a Friday in August he took up squatters residence in the abandoned Stop-n-Go. Two days later Aunt Darna drove up, parked by the office, her rusted station wagon mottled with jigsaw puzzle shapes of shadows cast by the sun through the oaks. She was inside talking to Mr. Buzzy for a few minutes. Sloop saw her there. He went about his workerly errands. He was an adult now and making a living and she could not drag him back like a child. He was at the pool checking the pH content when she found him.

Because Louise Murdo was across the pool, lying on her stomach, her bikini top undone, her thin body oiled a rich smooth brown the color of flowerpots. She lay on a green-and-white striped chaise lounge, atop a bright beach towel decorated gaily with a pattern of a toucan in jungle leaves, on the tiles near the chaise a can of Diet Coke, a pack of cigarettes, her butane lighter.

Aunt Darna spoke. "How you doing?" she asked.

"I'm fine." Sloop dumped a couple scoops of chlorine powder in to the tray that filtered it throughout the water, out through the jets. "And how are you?"

Darna stared at him for a minute. He met her eye to eye. He had nothing to hide. The sun made him squint. In the palm trees, the cicadas buzzed like joke handshakes. A pair of seagulls glided by. The sky was so blue you could not imagine an ounce of anguish or badness in the air.

Finally she said, "Peachy. I'm just peachy."

Sloop said, "That's good."

"Where you staying?" she asked. She stared at Louise as she asked this. Then she looked back at the auto court, the three cars in the parking lot, the oyster shell gravel gleaming white in the sun.

"I got a room here. It's not half bad."

Darna lit a cigarette and nodded. She began to walk away. Then stopped. "You ever coming back?"

Sloop could feel Louise listening. "Oh, I don't know," he said. "I don't know what I'm doing one minute to the next. You know what I mean? I just do it."

Darna nodded again. She looked exhausted, and it was barely past noon. "Well, you know you're welcome back, even just for din- ner or a snack or something. Okay?"

"I appreciate that."

Driving off, she honked once and waved.

Sloop scooped oleander leaves off the surface of the pool with the long-handled aluminum pole with blue mesh netting. Louise Murdo sat up, holding her top in place, then tying it carefully behind her back. She watched him work and smoked, sending plumes of gray menthol smell his way. She said, "You big fibber."

Sloop shrugged. "It don't matter anyway."

Louise rubbed lotion on her arms. "What'd you have for breakfast?"

"An old Snickers bar. There's still a few things left on the candy shelves in there, but I don't know." Sloop made a face. "Pretty stale."

"I'm going to get you some fried chicken and there's nothing you can do about it." She waited. "You hear that."

He kept scooping and wouldn't lift his head, wouldn't let her see his face.

—   —   —

Because in the jungle behind the courts, near 17, Sloop crouched in the bamboo thicket, waiting for Louise to take her afternoon shower. The sky turned dark as an open mouth above. Fat raindrops pattered on the wide banana tree leaves and palm fronds and spotted the gray concrete patio of the guest rooms. From the Murdos came the unexpected sound of doors being slammed and a sharp voice saying, "Well you goddamned well better find it." Noises of struggle, shovings, stumblings. The skirl of Louise's softer feminine voice pleading, begging, apologizing. A pause of quickened breathing and dread. Of powerlessness. The hope it was all over. Then more stumblings, the crunch of a door being kicked. The crying. George's voice shouting, "WHY DO YOU BRING THAT UP? HUH? WHY DO YOU BRING THAT UP? YOU WON'T EVER FORGET WILL YOU? YOU GO TO HELL. I MEAN IT. YOU GO TO HELL." Another door slammed. "YOU CALL YOURSELF A WIFE? IS THAT WHAT YOU THINK YOU ARE? WHAT A JOKE. WHAT A FUCKING JOKE."

Sloop was wet shivering as a stray, the stray that he was, his hair plastered pale to his pink forehead, cold rivulets trickling down his back, when Louise finally stepped into the bathroom, sobbing. He could not watch he could not stop himself. He tried closing his eyes. His knees ached from squatting for too long. She sat on the toilet in her underthings and cried for so long and so close to him from his perch in the bamboo that he could have reached out from the willowy knotted and knuckled green reeds and pinnate leaves and stroked her dark hair yellowed by the sun, the need for comforting human touch she so needed unbidden from another separate universe invisible, uncorporeal, ectoplastic.

— — —

By the pool, as Sloop cleaned it and lingered to hear her voice, to be near her, she talked. She spoke the truth. Her husband told one and all he was an equipment inspector and that was baloney. "That must be the seven-thousandth lie he's told about what he does. In Biloxi he was a flood insurance salesman and in Lake Charles he was a nutritionist. He always wants people to think he's something respectable, not the go-between for small-time low-life schemers that he is. Mostly he shuttles illegals off the boats from Mexico. I'm sure he's done worse, too. If you could look inside that man you'd shiver. I'm not kidding. And I'm married to him. I didn't know those things two years ago. I thought he was something. What a fool can be."

Sloop started to tell her about his theory of the pod people, how they're given props to make them seem human, like tubas and classic automobiles and cellular phones, and then, once they're close to you, they strike. But as he talked his voice grew fainter and fainter, until finally Louise said, "Well I don't know about all that but I suspect you're right on principle. He hoodwinked me, that's for sure."

— — —

Because the day on which Sloop emerged from fear into righteousness and justice was not one of brightness and light but one of spiderwebby grayness and a cloistered monkish feeling suffused with a smell of exotic incense or the perfume of a woman whose life will end in an untimely and unfortunate manner. It was November by then and the catfish fogs of autumn arrived in swirling billowing exhalation off the surface of the sea. The fog washed ashore in hovering waves, floating above the water in thick suspended strata. In wide banks it slowly settled upon the village and the motel. It eased whitely through the air, cascading over the red brick tiles of the motel like a viscous waterfall.

With the cool air of autumn the flocks of migrating waterfowl had arrived and were arriving daily and in the night blackness the bleating honks of Canada geese filling the velvet air loud and pleading confused and circling when the fog thickened opaque and moonlight swallowing driving them low to the ground to settle on the marshes just beyond the abandoned Stop-n-Go that Sloop now called a reluctant broken-glassed and graffiti-scrawled but unbothered unridiculed Home.

On that day of emergence and declaration the red-tiled roofs and stucco walls of The Sea Horse Motor Inn were crowded No Vacancy with birders. The Eighth Annual Christmas Beach Weekend of Waterfowl was in full swing, with bird enthusiasts from all over the state and beyond attending lectures at the Sand Dollar Pavilion, going on field trips, and attending photography seminars with experts like Hans Doerfmann and Helen Malyara. On the Sea Horse's pier impassioned voices whispered of sighting roseate spoonbills, American avocets, ruddy turnstones, and marbled godwits.

George Murdo sat by the pool and drank beers from an ice cooler. He offered some to a pair of newcomers but they said No thank you and drove away, the wife in the passenger side, eyes on a map, pretending he did not exist, thinking themselves better than him, rather, more responsible, unworried about creditors, deputy sheriffs with warrants, the Coast Guard, the DEA, the hell with them they don't know what it is to live to walk into Vegas with two grand in your pocket eager to lose or win free to do both.

He tried to joke with them. He told the couple as they were unloading their luggage Oh this place is just dandy, yes sir. Just dandy.

They change the sheets most every day. They do. But the question is How often do they change the fleas?

The woman looked as if he'd spit or as if she'd smelled something rotten which was attached to him. After they'd stepped inside 15 and closed the door, they pulled the curtains shut. On leaving George noticed them locking the door and checking it, twice.

Of course all it would take is a sharp bump with an elbow and howdy-do, that door would pop right open, the fools.

— — —

Because the fog seemed to have laid George low. To anyone who would listen he said they wouldn't be doing any oil-rig equipment inspecting today, by god. No sir. You can bet your life on that. That equipment would just have to inspect itself. Fog this thick you'd lose the bow of your boat and not find it till next February or March. He ranted and rambled to all and no one, one step above a homeless person or the disc jockey of a sorry-ass radio station.

Mr. Buzzy rubbed his weary bones his bloodshot eyes like that man would be the death of peace and told Sloop to keep an eye out that he didn't assault or batter any of the other guests, the high-paying, respectable sorts. He didn't want the Law over but if it came to that well so be it. Sloop said nothing. He drove the golf cart back toward the pool, hoping to catch a glimpse of Louise. She had not crossed the threshold of 17 in days. Last he'd seen her the bruises were still purple blue, galaxies of broken capillaries, most of her face though covered by the movie-star dark sunglasses, the wounded wasp queen alone in her hive.

George shouted into a cell phone. "I SAID I CAN'T DO IT, GODAMM-NIT! I'M IN NO CONDITION! Besides, I can't see shit. Not in this fog. I don't know what it's like where you are but over here it's so thick I can't see my dick with my pants down."

Late afternoon he passed out. All the other guests were gone, hunting for a glimpse of a whooping crane or a greater shearwater. A great blue heron landed on the store room roof right beside the pool but there were no birders there to see. Sloop walked up to George Murdo and he didn't stir an inch, dead to the world—a useless man passed out in public. Up this close he looked more like a pod person than Sloop had ever realized. His hair was artificially curled and unnaturally hued. His face was a queer shade of yellow-brown and his brows were grease-paint dark. He looked like a grotesque doll. A worthless doll won in an ugly carnival, smelling of beer and popcorn.

Sloop squatted close to him. He took the aluminum tubes of the chaise lounge in his hands. He lifted. The inert body was heavier than Sloop expected. But with a grunt and a heave, he jerked his side of the chaise high enough so that the slack unconscious blubbery bulk of George Murdo dumped into the pool, conking solidly on the tiled edge as it slumped into the water.

The surface of the pool sloshed with blue waves that stirred the mantle of fog. Sloop swallowed and glanced around, but there was not another human present. The heron flapped heavily away, long legs dangling.

Sloop moved to the edge and peered into the water, watching as George's mouth gulped water, his head shook and arms legs shoulders exploded into spastic motion. Twisting this way and that like a carp on a line, a bottom feeder caught and yanked to the light of day. He pushed toward the surface, struggling against a great blue crush.

As if no more than the left hand of god Sloop reached into the water and caught George's head as it was about to surface, and leaning over, on his knees, amid the strong spicy smell of chlorine and the chilly opacity of the muffling fog, he held the hard wet skin of George's skull and scalp as it twitched and lurched. At one point a yellow shocked hand broke the surface. Sloop knelt and cupped the slimy scalp until it stopped moving. He had once been on a pier and asked by a fisherman if he wanted to touch a hammerhead and doing that felt something like this. Until it stopped moving completely.

George sank slowly toward the bottom.

Sloop brushed the water off his wet arm and stood to take up the long-handled net. He didn't know what to do with that, though, and after staring at the body in the water for several minutes, and once bumping it with the net, he shuffled over to the office. Inside, he told the manager there was a problem with the man in 17.

Mr. Buzzy sighed and turned down the TV set. "What now?"

Sloop said maybe he should come see. The man was in the pool but he didn't look like he was diving for dollars. Or whatever he was searching for he wouldn't be finding. Leastways not in this lifetime.

— — —

Because there was no actual funeral. George Murdo was cremated and Louise scattered the ashes in Red Moon Bay because it was cheaper that way you didn't have to pay for a god-awful expensive coffin she was a single woman on her own the money was better spent on new clothes or food for the living and not a fancy wooden box for the dead and good-riddanced.

There was a memorial service. Held in the small pavilion at Carter's Landing, it was attended only by Louise, Mr. Buzzy, George's hair stylist from Hair You Go Again, and Sloop. A solemn tall preacherman in a baby blue suit with a red carnation in his lapel said George was a good man. No one bothered to argue.

They drove home and went back to life. Sloop caught a ride with Louise in George's huge stylish mermaid-green Bel Air she'd never been allowed to drive before. They walked to the end of The Sea Horse's fishing pier and watched the sea sneak in below the fog.

Beneath them, the waves were dead. Black skimmers passed by, wing beats holding them low to the water, only their orange bills breaking a vee in the placid surface. The air smelled of the rotting bleached pier, the railings spattered with the droppings of gulls. Across Pelican Avenue the neon emerald-and-amber sea horse sign shimmered faintly, ethereal, a lovely glowing question mark through the fog.

In the long silence Sloop thought to speak. He had it all planned out. What he would say. Or spoke in thought. Not aloud. He told her he had done it. He rehearsed the lines: I want you to know that. I'm not a sneak. I did it and I'm not proud but I did it. I put him in the water. I held him down. He quit moving.

Louise listened to the silence, to the metal clang of buoys in the fog, the cry of sea birds. She squinted and stared into Sloop's eyes and mind and thoughts and beyond down to his soul. She smoked a cigarette and leaned softly against him. She sensed he must be thinking of his mother, his father, whatever kept this boy in his head so much. When he started to speak, she watched only his lips.

"I held him—." His voice broke hoarse, his mouth convulsing.

"Hush," said Louise. She put a warm hand to his neck and pulled him to touch her chest. "Now you hush that."

He mumbled into her throat. He told her he couldn't. It was the pod people, you see. They were taking over the world. They killed his mother and they killed his father and he had to do something. He couldn't just stand there. He had to. "Can't you see? Tell me you can see."

"I can see," she said. "I can see without words."

"I looked at you, too. I did."

"Hush that." She hugged him and kissed his quivering eyelids. "Because it's time to be quiet now."

# Playboys

Lennon is in his bedroom, blowing at a cup of beef bouillon to cool it off, wearing a white terry cloth bathrobe. He drinks steaming bouillon for lunch every day. "It flushes out the kidneys," he tells Jennifer, poking his side.

"How romantic," she says. Jennifer is half-dressed, sitting on the bed. Lennon insists he's telling the truth about his kidneys, and explains that he drank bouillon every afternoon in Argentina, while climbing the Andes.

"The highest mountain in the western hemisphere is down there. It's huge." He stretches one arm over his head. "Really. Over twenty-two thousand feet." A quilt is draped over the window to darken the room. Jennifer fluffs her short hair with her fingertips, and in the dim light, her shaven underarms and small breasts seem unusually white. "I slipped and almost fell in a giant crevasse."

Jennifer nods uh huh. She puts on her rings, fastens her clear plastic Swatch. "I bet you're making this up," she says. Jennifer is still married, but her husband moved out of their house, after having an affair because she wouldn't make love to him. Whenever he tried, she'd say, "I can't. I have cramps." Now, she sees Lennon three or four times a week. Now, she tastes the bouillon on his mouth when they kiss with their tongues.

There's a glass ashtray beside Jennifer on the rumpled blue sheets of the bed, and she smokes exactly half a cigarette, carefully tapping off the ashes. "Where'd you get that robe?" she asks, smiling. "You look like the Aqua Velva man." Jennifer is short but muscular, think gymnast. Her bangs reach to her eyebrows, and she has sweeping arcs of straight, dark hair meeting at her chin. She has come over for lunch sex and now it's time to go. "I better get dressed," she says. "Or Mr. Pfeiffer is going to kill me." She hooks her bra together around her waist, then twists it around and wriggles into the white straps, as Lennon watches, wondering what he's going to do for the rest of the day. "You know what I go through for you. I'm supposed to have cafeteria patrol today, but I traded with Wendy Lopez, the Home Ec lady. She's a natural at that kind of thing."

"What's cafeteria patrol?"

"You don't know anything, you know that?" She sits on Lennon's lap and musses his hair. "Did anyone ever tell you that, in a certain light, you're kind of cute?"

"Stop. You're just trying to get on my good side."

"I am." After several kisses, Jennifer drives to the high school where she teaches drama. It's late spring in Denver, and the mountains to the west are bruised with thunderstorms and fire. Raindrops dapple the windshield. A blast of cold air shakes her car, and Jennifer feels full of Lennon, feels him leaking out of her. Her husband's name is Foster. Foster Foster Foster. He sells neckties, and knows a good deal when he sees one. As he told Jennifer on their honeymoon. He pointed at her and said, "I know a good deal when I see one."

— – —

Foster is in Neiman Marcus, waiting for his favorite salesgirl, hands in his pockets, smoothing two coins between his right thumb and index finger. He's trying hard not to look at the nearly nude models on pantyhose packages. He hums. Cindy Anderson, the blonde salesgirl who has toyed with his heart for long enough, is processing a customer's American Express card. As she inserts the carbon copy charge slip into her cash register, Cindy has a brief but powerful mental image of Foster as a dog begging for scraps at a dinner table, his black nose resting on the table cloth, whimpering. Her friend Rebecca, who works in Cosmetics, disapproves of Foster. "You know what you are to him? The Insignificant Other." She says Foster's just using her as a sexual surrogate for his wife, to bolster his sense of self-worth and to dispel his feelings of inadequacy. Cindy thinks she might have a point. Foster strolls over to a triptych of full-length mirrors and checks his hair. From there he sees beneath the saloon doors of the women's dressing room. A skirt drops, legs step out of it. "Did you want me?" asks Cindy.

"Do I want you?" Foster grins. "Well, you might say that."

"Ha ha." Cindy's eye shadow is dusky blue to match her irises. She blinks and arches her eyebrows, waiting. She's wearing Obsession again today, and hopes Foster doesn't notice and make that same tired joke. You could read a paper through his charm. Whenever Cindy now thinks of sex with Foster, she thinks of baby powder. He puts it on his body after every shower. "It absorbs the sweat," he told her. Once she noticed how powder-white his toes were, as if they'd been dusted by blackboard erasers. After making love to him, she always feels like there's a ring of baby powder around her mouth.

Foster asks if she wants to have lunch. "You name it. I'm buying."

"No," she says, straightening a rack of pastel negligees. "No, I don't think so, Foster."

"Why not?"

"Number one, I think we're seeing too much of each other.

Number two, maybe we should cool it a little. And number three, I need some space. You know what I'm saying, Foster?"

"Okay. Sure. No problem." Foster nods, and steps back. "No biggee."

— — —

Jennifer returns from lunch in faded jeans, white sneakers, and her black leather jacket, smoking another cigarette. She knows she should quit but she hates the idea of jumping on the bandwagon with every stair-master junkie in the universe. Besides, she's not like Joan Crawford or anything. As she's walking down the hall, one of her jokey ex-students says, "Can I see your hall pass?" She makes a face at him. Rachel Keating is waiting for her at the auditorium where they're holding rehearsals for a production of J. M. Synge's *Playboy of the Western World*. Rachel is a senior who has the female lead in *Playboy,* and she's also Jennifer's friend. "Guess what," she says. "Gina Bartholemew has mono. There goes our Widow Quinn."

Jennifer sighs and slumps against an auditorium door. "How'd she get that? Making out?"

"Who knows. But I think you should take the part. No way anyone else is going to learn the lines in time."

Jennifer nods. "Maybe it's for the best. But don't quote me, okay? Gina's accent was the pits."

"I *knew* you agreed with me. Even though you wouldn't admit it."

Jennifer smiles. "The word is 'tact.'" She sits down in the front row and tells the students to start with Act One, since that's still weak. Jennifer calls out, "We don't want to bomb in the first few minutes, now do we?" Kyle Carter and Bradley Hodges, who play Christy Mahon and Shawn Keogh, take their places on the dusty hardwood stage. They drag out two stools and sit down, holding their photocopied scripts. Brad acts as if he's going to spit on him. "You better not," says Kyle. "You do and you'll be sorry." Brad swallows, making a face.

Brad and Rachel read their lines, with Jennifer correcting their Irish accents. Behind them is a backdrop of fire escapes and streetlamps, left over from *West Side Story*. Jennifer is still warm and wobbly from making love, but reminds herself she is Mrs. Powell, sitting in an empty auditorium of the Susan B. Anthony School for the Performing Arts, teaching teenagers how to act. Does it matter that she had Lennon for lunch? What she does in her spare time is her business, right? The kids on stage keep muffing their lines and wisecracking. "Hey you guys!" she calls out. "What is this, amateur hour? You better get it in gear!" Three girls behind the curtain, who play local flirts that come on stage late in Act One, mimic her. "Amateur hour! Amateur hour!"

"You won't think it's so funny when you're up there dying in front of the entire planet!"

Next they rehearse the comic scene where Christy confesses to killing his father. Kyle and Brad do a good job with the timing of their lines, while Rachel drops her script and speaks from memory, going through her movements on the stage. For a moment at least, everything is under Jennifer's control.

Alone on his lunch hour, Foster orders a hamburger at McDonald's, the teenage workers all wearing headsets with microphones. He has the uneasy feeling that this is Mission Control at NASA.

Lennon places a copper-bottomed two-quart sauce pan on the stove and turns the black knob. The blue flame bursts into life with a soft, velvety whoosh. He rubs his nose and rereads the morning paper as he waits for it to boil. There is going to be no easy way to tell Jennifer he's leaving Denver to go mountain climbing all summer. "Go ahead and go," she'll say, "but don't expect me to wait for you." After the water comes to a boil Lennon turns off the flame and drops in the tube of mink oil, folding it to immerse the whole thing.

He spreads newspaper across the kitchen table, puts his boots up on it, then removes the rawhide laces. The hot water has softened the waxy yellow mink oil, and squeezing some of it onto a rag, he works it into the dark leather of the climbing boots, coating the stitches especially. You've got to seal your boots to keep feet dry and warm on muddy days, say, in the fog and mist of Patagonia. Jennifer will have to realize why he's going and be a good sport. The boots are new, a birthday present from her. "I can't believe you've actually climbed mountains with those old clodhoppers you wear," she told him. "I just bought you these so you wouldn't break your neck."

For six years now he's been taking classes at the University of Denver and has tried his hand at several majors. He finally moved out of his grandparents' house, and is living off student loans. Now he's decided to become a mountain climber. He bought a pair of crampons and a coil of climbing rope, but he still hasn't done any serious climbing, just the easiest routes of the peaks outside Boulder.

Jennifer thinks Lennon's problem is that he smokes too much pot. She calls him Sleepyhead because he's always yawning. And one of his secret and most despairing fears is that he will never be truly awake, alive, before slipping into some irreversible deep sleep. After making a cup of coffee, he slaps his cheeks and clears his throat. He feels guilty about lying to Jennifer about the Andes. The farthest south he ever traveled was a road trip to Guadalajara. He was supposed to go all the way to the black sand beaches of Oaxaca, but he got sick and had to come back early, driving across two thousand miles of desert with his bloodstream full of amoebas.

– – –

After work, Foster stops at a supermarket. He is struck by the essential humiliation of it, buying your own food to take home to your small housing unit to feed yourself. When you're alone, it's not like cooking, he thinks. It's like feeding the cat. Only the cat is you. He thinks that everyone is staring at him. In the express checkout line at the supermarket, surrounded by magazines, razor blades, and butane lighters, Foster adds a TV guide and chocolate bar to his seven items, feeling guilty about it. On the wall at the end of the checkout line are stuffed heads of moose and bighorn sheep. Even they seem to be watching him. His ears are ringing. He looks into the future and sees a cold and tacky apartment full of clock radios and despair.

The ringing in his ears, tinnitus, is from a hunting accident. A friend's rifle went off too close to Foster's left ear. Was it really an accident? Could it have been a sign? The ringing keeps him up at night, especially now that he sleeps alone, and is trapped with his own thoughts, without the aloe vera scent of Jennifer's skin. His head no longer fits on the pillow. And under the constant ringing is the hygienic lifelessness of his unfurnished condo. He sometimes turns on the garbage disposal just to break the stillness. The woman in the line ahead of him has twelve items. Sixteen, if you count the lemons individually. Who does she think she is?

Foster is the manager of the men's department of Neiman Marcus. He believes the three main skills of effective managerial technique are discipline, diplomacy, and dread. But Foster is never going to amount to anything and he knows it, as well as he knows they are going to have to ship back most of those Ralph Lauren shirts they have had for over two months now because people just don't like them. Maybe that's his problem, too. People just don't like him.

He used to believe in himself. He makes a good salary and drives a Honda Element. People used to admire and respect him. Then one night while they were having dinner at a friend's house, Jennifer—his own wife! she should be on his team!—mentioned off hand that all salesmen were basically scum. "I used to be a salesman," said Foster. "In fact, I still am a salesman, kind of."

"Oh, I wasn't talking about you, Foster. I was talking about all those other guys." She waved her hand in the air, indicating the rest of the salesmen in the world. She'd had too much wine. She went on to say that most salesmen, the kind that pressure people into buying things they don't want, should be shot and fed to crocodiles. "I mean, they really don't provide any service. They don't build a computer chip or find a cure for emphysema. They just push push push. They don't care if you need the product or not or if it's junk or not. They just want their commission. They're drains on society."

Foster asked, "What has gotten into you?"

Later Jennifer told him, "I just can't, honey. I think I'm about to start my period." Foster couldn't sleep. He lay in bed, staring at the miniblind shadows on the wall. He wondered why Jennifer was always bleeding.

When he moved out, Foster felt himself turn into a bullfrog. He grew huge and warty and could no longer speak, but only croak. He still went to work every morning, but his employees laughed and pointed at him. They refused to obey any of his commands. At lunch they put firecrackers in his wide froggy mouth and watched him explode. In the checkout line at the supermarket, he imagines swatting the lemon woman in the back of her head with his long sticky tongue.

—  —  —

On Saturday, Jennifer hammers homemade signs onto the telephone poles at intersections near her house: DIVORCE SALE! EVERYTHING MUST GO! She places a wardrobe rack of Foster's old clothes on the new grass of the front lawn, and puts a row of boxes on the sidewalk. She coils up the green garden house and disconnects the sprinkler. Then she fills the yard with Fosterana. Her students show up early, since she'd been talking about the divorce sale all week. Rachel rummages through a pile of paperbacks and asks which ones are the juiciest. When Lennon walks out with a box of clothes, she says Hi.

She and Jennifer talk on the phone almost every night, and she knows all about their affair. Sometimes, when Jennifer returns from lunch, Rachel smiles and says, "Did we just have love in the afternoon?" Before Jennifer slept with Lennon, she told Rachel about him, how he was two years younger. "Stop the presses," said Rachel. "What a shocker." Jennifer also confessed she felt kind of rusty—in a sexual way—and asked what she would do. Rachel said, "If I were you?"

"If you were me."

"Go for it. Definitely."

Kyle, Brad, and Jonathan Schilling show up at the yard sale, arguing which is better, USC or UCLA. They fight over one of Foster's old camping knives with an antler horn handle. "Hey!" says Jennifer. "Knock it off before you kill somebody." Jennifer tells Rachel she read a book of letters J. M. Synge wrote to Molly Allgood, the actress who originally played Pegeen Mike, the lead in *Playboy*, and about how sweet the letters were. "He called her 'Dearest Pet' and 'Dearest Life.' Isn't that sweet?"

Rachel pulls back her long red hair and works it into a hair-tie. "Sounds kind of gushy to me."

"But sometimes gushy is good, don't you think?"

While Jennifer is talking with Rachel, Foster drives up. He gets out of the car and shuts the door. He keeps his hands in his pockets and stares at the row of clothes, his old TV, the gun rack he built in the ninth grade. He nods to Jennifer when he sees she's watching him, but does not acknowledge Lennon, who is completely oblivious to the fact that Foster hates every cell in his body and would gladly rip his heart out. Foster squats in front of the box of records and flips through them casually, sometimes stopping for a moment to read the song titles or the liner notes on the back, once slipping the black vinyl disk out to cradle it with his thumb and middle finger.

He picks up the entire box and brings it to Jennifer. "Who said you could sell this stuff? It's mine."

"I'm tired of it taking up space."

"I said I was going to pick it up."

Jennifer straightens the stack of paperbacks in a cardboard box. "You never acted like you wanted any of it, anyway. Until now."

Brad walks up and asks, "Mrs. Powell, how much do you want for this old tent?"

"That's mine," says Foster. "My wife has no right to sell that."

"As far as I'm concerned, Foster, we're not married anymore."

Brad looks inside the stuff sack. "It doesn't look like it's got all the pieces, anyway."

"It doesn't," says Foster. "It's a piece of junk. Like all this stuff."

Lennon is sitting on a folding metal chair at a table of men's ties, yard tools, and fishing equipment. In front of him is a yellow plastic bucket for live bait, a spool of monofilament line, a green tackle box with white compartments open to show the artificial eyes and fins inside. He ignores Foster, even when he overhears him ask what exactly that jerk is doing, selling *my* clothes.

"Don't start, okay?"

"Right. I don't need any of this junk, anyway. It all looks rather pathetic, doesn't it?"

"I don't think you should come around here anymore. You've really ruined everything, you know that? I'm sorry. Really, Foster. I'm sorry. But I don't like seeing you or being around you anymore."

Foster nods. He walks to his car and opens the door, stands for a moment as if he's forgotten something. He gets in and starts the car, but before he drives away, he leaves the motor running, yanks up the emergency brake handle, and gets back out. He walks over to Jennifer. "Can't we be friends?" He nods at her, as if to make her say yes. He smiles awkwardly. "I don't remember you always being a bitch."

"Do you want me to hate you? Is that it?"

"Oh, just forget it," he says. He gets back in his car and revs the engine. "Have a nice life!" he shouts.

After Foster leaves, Jennifer goes into the house and returns with a drawer full of silverware. "Look at all this junk!" she says as she walks across the yard. "Doesn't anyone want any of it?" She walks up to Brad and Kyle. "What about some spoons? Want some spoons, Brad?"

"I don't know," he says. Jennifer is wearing a white buttondown cotton shirt, with the tails hanging out, and through a gap between the buttons, Brad catches a glimpse of her breasts. That makes it hard for him to think. "My mom's got plenty of 'em."

Jennifer sets the silverware tray down on the table with the ties, the fishing tackle. She holds a fork in the air. "How many times you figure Foster put this in his mouth?"

"Let me guess," says Kyle. "Two zillion."

Jennifer shakes her head, and says, "Too many."

Brad pokes at them as if he might buy one. "Then why'd you ever marry him?"

—　—　—

Why why why? He had a dimple in his chin, like Kirk Douglas. He taught her to snow ski. In college, he was a business major, but nobody's perfect, right? He was actually, truly a funny person. He was an early riser, and every morning, when they were first married, she would feel him rub the soles of her bare feet before he left for school, like a World War Two pilot tapping a pin-up before a bombing run.

But once he reached the real world, he changed. He became stuffo—a stodgebox. He gained weight and refused to buy larger size slacks, because he didn't want to admit he was getting chubby. His pants were often so tight his stomach made noises. This drove Jennifer up the wall. "Did you hear that?" she'd ask.

"Hear what?"

After a while, he never told her how beautiful she was, as he used to. When she was leaving for the audition for the lead in 'night, Mother, at the Franklin Street Playhouse, Foster said, "Good luck." Not as if he were wishing her luck to get the part, but as if he wished she'd wake up and smell the coffee. As if to say, don't kid yourself, Jen. You're *not* that good.

Finally, after she found out about Cindy Anderson, Jennifer told him they had to have a talk. She admitted that she thought that well maybe the best thing for both of them would be if he found a new place to live. "I'm sorry, Foster. I think this is over." He refused to react. "I still love you, but more like a brother or an uncle now," she said. She sighed, turning her coffee cup around in a circle. "I don't know," she added. "Maybe, more like a cousin." Foster nodded. He wouldn't—and couldn't—look at her. He leafed through a book called *Denizens of the Deep.* He turned to a page that showed a man on a hospital operating table with his right leg bitten off by a great white shark. "Would you look at that," he said. When she didn't answer, he looked up from the page and said, "I'm sorry." He closed the book. "Well," he said, and stared at his hands. "So."

—   —   —

A week after the yard sale, it's opening night. Lennon has to park on a side street. The high school parking lot is full. As he walks to the auditorium, he follows a mother sparkling with jewelry and a father in a dark suit, their sons hurrying ahead, neckties loose around their lapels. It's a cool evening, with a bright moon above and black fir trees all around. There's the sound of people shutting their car doors, and the gravel crunches loudly as they have to walk on the shoulder of the road. As Lennon gets closer to the school, more and more people fill the roadside. Latecomers drive slowly through the rows of people walking toward the high school, their headlights shining on the families, bathing mothers in bright light, fathers in shadow.

Inside, ushers in red sports jackets direct people to their seats and hand out playbills. Lennon holds the blue paper in his hands and reads, like everyone else. Welcome to the Susan B. Anthony High School for the Performing and Visual Arts production of J. M. Synge's *Playboy of the Western World*. A Tragi-Comedy in Three Acts. Directed by Jennifer Powell. There will be a ten-minute intermission. Special thanks to Kwik Copies and Frizetti's Dry Cleaning for their support.

Lennon forgets to remove his blue down vest before the play begins, and he's too warm, but doesn't want to distract anyone with his movement. Sweat begins to prickle his stomach and back. He sits in the middle of the auditorium, next to a teenage girl wearing huge hooped earrings, blue jean jacket, and black tights. Her hair is filled with tiny waves from a crimping iron. She catches Lennon looking at her, and stares back at him, her Cleopatra eyes focused on Lennon's mouth.

Foster arrives late. His ear, nose, and throat doctor has prescribed sodium pentothal to treat the tinnitus, and he wears a round band-aid-like patch behind his right ear. "Isn't that truth serum?" he asked, when the doctor gave him the prescription. "Not for you." So far, it hasn't helped the ringing, but only nauseated him. His hair follicles tingle fiercely. He has to sit in the back of the auditorium, near the doors.

The ushers stand behind him with flashlights, once the play begins, to lead latecomers to the last few seats available. It's hard for him to hear back there, especially over the ringing in his ears. The woman in front of him is wearing too much perfume, and as he crosses his legs, he hits the back of her seat. She turns around in her chair and frowns. He's so far from the stage that he doesn't recognize Jennifer immediately, when she comes on stage near the end of Act One.

As Foster is momentarily fooled by her costume of peasant dress, rouged cheeks, and gray wig, Jennifer also becomes immersed in her character. She unfolds in it, cracks her cocoon of denial, and emerges onstage, all emotions intact, her bright wings delicate and moist. She plays off Rachel, who speaks her lines in a rich Irish accent and is sexy in her low-cut dress and brightly painted cheeks. Rachel flings her hair about like a banshee, dominating stage left, letting the other actors feed off her energy. By the middle of Act One their comic timing clicks—the audience laughs in the right moments, and the actors loosen up, encouraged by success.

Although Lennon is caught up in the play, watching Jennifer reminds him of South America and the lies he's told. He knows of Zurbriggen's famous climb of Aconcagua in 1897, when they scaled the Horcones glacier with primitive equipment like silk sleeping bags and hemp ropes. He remembers reading how they had to melt the frozen lumps of grease in their Irish stew with the heat of their mouths. At nearly 22,000 feet they built a meager fire of wood brought up from below, and ended up drinking wine and coffee all night, shivering and crying like children from the cold.

These were the same mountains Lennon had boasted of climbing. And at first his mountaineering exploits had simply been, what? Poetic exaggeration? But somewhere along the way, especially since he has fallen in love with Jennifer, the lie has broken out of its cage. Every waking hour of his drowsy existence he can feel it now, somewhere at his back, following him. He can no longer even enjoy the touch of Jennifer's bee-sting lips.

At intermission between Acts One and Two Lennon and Foster both use the men's room at the same time. Lennon rinses his hands and splashes water on his face to wake up. He doesn't notice

Foster standing behind him, his reflection in the mirror. Foster also washes his hands. There's a scent of baby powder in the air. Lennon slaps the hot air hand dryer and, as it whirs to life, he realizes who that is in the mirror. He acts as if he doesn't recognize Foster, and keeps his head averted, staring intently at the hot air hand dryer mounted on the wall. He knows Foster is watching him, but doesn't want to meet his eyes. He wonders what his problem is, anyway. I'm not the one who left his wife. Foster stands behind him, his hands wet, wondering when the jerk is going to quit rubbing his hands. He considers slamming Lennon's head against the wall.

As Lennon walks back to his seat, he feels Foster tailing him closely, until he steps out of the aisle and has to squeeze past the teenage girls to reach his seat.

On stage, near the end of Act Two, Jennifer plays the old Irish widow with emotion. She jabs her finger at Rachel, who has her hands on her hips, her red hair tousled and swept to one side, hanging across her chest. Kyle Carter, who plays the male lead, enjoys the spotlight on his part, and seems to revel in both Jennifer and Rachel fighting over him in the play, alternating in his role between swaggering charmer and meek young man. It's a smooth combination of imagination and reality.

Foster sits at the rear of the auditorium, his spine sore from resting against the wooden back of his seat. He can't get comfortable in this world anymore! He has neglected to shave, wash, or brush his teeth the last few days and his tie is knotted anyhow under his stubbly chin and guilty adam's apple, his collar unbuttoned. He has an erection. He imagines Jennifer at his funeral, her saying I really loved him I just didn't know how to tell him that. I didn't know he was so depressed. If I had, I would have done something. I would have clasped him in my arms and loved him as he should have been loved. Love? You don't know what the word means are you kidding me? All you love is yourself you're selfish you know that? It's always you you you.

Near the end of Act Three, a crowd of student extras in Irish peasant outfits come on stage to jeer at Kyle. Rachel stands at stage left, disgusted with the hero when he turns out not to be the man he claimed he was. Foster leaves the auditorium and walks to his car. There is a ring around the moon now, and it is higher in the sky. He gets on Interstate 70 heading for the winding mountain roads near Idaho Springs and Georgetown. He's just going for a drive in the country. To get some air. Nothing unusual. He's going for a drive, to see what he can see. People do it all the time. Fifty thousand Americans are killed every year in traffic accidents. A nice shining car, a few drinks, a mountain road—a combination ending in death. When they interview the victim's wife she says, I loved him. God, he'll never know how much I always loved him.

The last scene of the play is tense. The audience is quiet. In her character as the Irish widow, Jennifer tries to fasten a petticoat around Kyle, to save him from the police by disguising him as a woman. He pushes her away, then grabs a shovel and acts as if he'll bash in her head. She runs offstage, and once she's behind the set door, stops to catch her breath. Everyone is crowded together back there, watching the play through gaps in the plywood walls of the set. One of the students pats Jennifer's sweaty back as she tosses off the wool shawl that was part of her costume. She fans herself with a playbill someone hands her, and peeks through a crack to watch the ending. The play is beautiful! She hopes Lennon saw it. One of the stagehands taps Jennifer on the shoulder, and when she turns and squints at him in the dim light, he draws back his upraised hand in the air, offering her a high five.

Lennon rises and makes his way awkwardly down the row of seats. The play is in its final moments. Kyle swaggers offstage to laughter, pushing Jonathan Schilling, who plays his father, through the set door. Rachel stamps her foot, tugs histrionically at her hair, and boxes Bradley Hodges on the ear. The teenage girls frown at Lennon and hold up their feet or turn sideways in their seats to let him pass, while he's thinking that maybe this isn't the best timing in the world but he has to split, like, now. Later alligator. He's leaving for South America that day, that night, immediately-if-not-sooner. He'll call Jennifer from Buenos Aires. Won't that be a hoot?

He finally reaches the aisle as the stage lights fade to black. Many miles away, Foster slows the car as he swings through the dead man's curve and holds onto his miserable life with both hands. Things could be worse, he tells himself. Think of the starving children in Africa. After making his way down the aisle, Lennon steps through the thick velvet curtains behind the red exit sign and tries to leave. But it's so dark he can't see. The doors seem locked and won't open, or perhaps he's just pushing the bar the wrong way. As he tries pulling at it and struggling with it he becomes aware of a sound erupting behind him, as if a huge flock of birds with human hands for wings has suddenly taken off, bursting the air with wild applause.

# Warsaw, 1984

After the first day, when we moved into the apartment in Warsaw, I seldom saw Tomasz. While he was visiting family and friends I was stranded, afraid to go out on my own, afraid I'd be murdered by one of the drunken factory workers who weaved on the sidewalk near the door of our building. They all had patches on their eyes or bloody lips from fighting. One day as I passed them on the sidewalk—hurrying back to the apartment, hoping to god the key worked—I heard something crunch beneath my shoe and, quickly looking down, I noticed it was someone's bloody teeth. They had apparently just been spit out by a thin, wrinkled man, leaning against the wall, gurgling into his hand. The corneas of his eyes were a bright yellow, and he was blocking the way, staring at me.

"Studenty?" he asked. I nodded quickly, then he smiled and bowed, swinging one arm towards the door in a be-my-guest. He kicked the air behind me as I scurried by, missing me.

By the fourth day I had my Eurrail map out and was imagining all the other places I could be.

"Greece is supposed to be beautiful," I told Tadek. He was an old friend of Tomasz's who was taking care of me.

"What you need is woman," he said, pouring a shot of vodka at ten in the morning. He had a long face with droopy brown eyes that were always bloodshot. His teeth were yellow and mossy, and his dark Stalinesque mustache hung over his lips. We had rolls and butter for breakfast each morning and his mustache held the crumbs and drops of honey long after we had eaten. He chased the honey down with vodka. His motto was *do pić, do ruchać, i radio do słuchać*: To drink, to fuck, and to listen to the radio.

At the end of breakfast he crossed his legs and lit a cigarette. "Tonight we go party."

She was pretty, married, and the only girl at the party who spoke English. The room was full of smoke and we all downed glasses of cold vodka at once, on the common toast,

"Na zdrowie!"

I wasn't sure what the party was for but it seemed like a wake. The living room in the apartment was small and full of people. At the end of the couch a man sat wrapped in a plaid wool blanket, with a Dachshund sitting on his chest. It kept licking his face with its eelish pink tongue.

"His mother died yesterday," said Tadek. "He is depressed."

"Who's the girl in the blue dress? She's cute."

He stood up on his tiptoes to get a better look at whom I was talking about. "Her?" Then he smiled.

Tadek told me all about her. He pointed out her husband, who looked like a young Kojak, thick and stocky, his head a fleshy, taut dome, his forehead lined.

"Why'd she marry him?" I asked.

Tadek shrugged. "Maybe she was hungry." He told me she had lived in New York, when her father had been a diplomat with the Polish embassy.

"Spy," he whispered.

She kept smiling at me so I moved close to her in the crowded room. "Tadek says you speak English," I said.

She shook her head. "I do not know how to speak English. He must be thinking of someone else. I am good Polish girl."

"I bet."

"Seriously. Do you have cigarette?" I gave her one, then couldn't find any matches. She took my hand and led me into the kitchen.

"They are mad at your friend."

She was talking about Tomasz. He was saying Poland was a mess, that it was never going to solve its problems and everyone should just face it. It was always going to be this awful. He said the smartest and best people were leaving Poland and soon only the idiots and peasants would be left. He'd had too much vodka. She told me a couple of the men at the party whom Tomasz had never met were listening and wanted to beat him up.

"He is traitor. He thinks he is better than us."

"Maybe I should warn him," I said.

"No." She leaned against me, touching my arm. "It is not your battle. Right?" We were crowded into the kitchen and she had shut the door to the rest of the apartment. She wore a sleeveless dress, and I felt the cool skin of her arms against mine.

"I have enough vodka," she said. "I want tea." I was close enough to her to smell the pale hair at the nape of her neck, fine and curly. She burned her right hand lighting the pilot light in the oven with a wooden match, then sucked the fingertips and shook her head.

"Why am I lighting this?" she asked, pointing at the oven. "We want this thing," she pointed at the burner on the stove. "For tea. You are causing me to mistake," she said, and smiled, looking at her burned fingers.

The steam hissed out of the pot. "I wish you weren't married."

"Why?"

"Because we might, you know . . . I don't know. Go out or something." She sipped her tea and looked at the door. It had a rippled pane of glass in it, which distorted the figures of the people in the other room, and wobbly human shapes passed by.

"We can go out," she said, and dumped all the matches out of the paper box, then wrote her phone number inside. The door opened and one of her friends came in looking for her. She slipped the empty book of matches in my shirt pocket and whispered in my ear to call only during the daytime.

— — —

The next day Tadek and I traveled by tram across town to see a British film that would have Polish subtitles. When we got there the theater was closed. There was a handwritten sign on the door.

"What does it say?"

"Projectionist is dead." We went to a restaurant and the waitress told us the cook was sick so there was only cold chicken and tea. Tadek laughed so hard he coughed and his face turned bright red. The tablecloth was splotched wine purple and cigarette-ash gray. We drank shots of vodka from a small bottle.

The man sitting next to us asked, "Is the vodka good?"

We gave him a drink. It was raining outside, gray and chilly June weather. Tadek was reading a Polish paper that had a smattering of international news. The man we were sharing vodka with squeezed my knee and leaned against me, his awful breath in my face, and I couldn't understand a thing he was saying. Tadek checked the weather reports in Paris and Amsterdam. He smiled and said, "In the west, the sun is shining."

— — —

Two days later I called Helena. She sounded glad to hear from me and said Yes, could we meet and go for a walk? She was just taking her baby out for some fresh air.

"Baby?"

"Is that problem?" she said. "You do not like babies?"

"No no, that's fine. I just didn't know you had one."

She wore dark sunglasses and a gray sweatshirt with an appliqué Snoopy on the front. She pushed a baby carriage down a cracked, wet sidewalk. The sun was behind clouds and its grayish light cast no shadows through the elms and maples along the street.

"It is me," she said, smiling as she raised the glasses. "I am nervous. I am sweating." She pulled the sweatshirt out from her body. "This is Wojtek."

Wojtek was eight months old, a fat little monster with his father's wide forehead, dull baby eyes, and drool on his lips. He started crying when he saw me. His tiny stiff fingers seemed to point at me, accusingly, as he wailed.

"Cute baby," I said.

"You want to hold?"

"No. I might drop it."

"He is not it."

We followed the cracks of the sidewalk to a small park. It was full of trees, narrow walkways of red sand, and small plots of gardens where short, fat women with kerchiefs on their heads tended flowers. They leaned on hoes and smiled as we passed, looking at baby Wojtek if they were close enough. One of them was admiring him and pointing at me, smiling, her huge hands wrinkled and knotty. Helena laughed and said the women thought Wojtek had my eyes. I shook my head and started to say something, but Helena whispered, "Do not talk."

Other women pushed baby carriages in the park, but Helena was the only one accompanied by a man. It began to rain again, huge drops plopping on the glossy back hood of the carriage. We hurried beneath a tree, shaking raindrops out of our hair.

"Let us sit here to wait out rain," said Helena. There wasn't much dry space beneath the branches of the tree and we huddled together. I put my arm around her awkwardly and looked about, to see if we were being watched. The park was frowsy, with bottle caps along the walkway, and cigarette butts scattered among the roots of the tree. Helena drew words in the dirt between the roots, Polish words that I couldn't understand. When I asked what they were, she said, "Look them up in your dictionary." She was referring to my Berlitz *Polish for Travelers*—1200 Phrases, 2000 Useful Words. She thought it was funny.

"Would you like to have a drink?" she said, mimicking the phrases in the "Making Friends" section. "Oh, and here is even better one: 'Are you on your own?'" She looked at me and, after seeing my feelings were hurt, pushed my knee and laughed, showing her small white teeth. "You worry too much."

She left her hand on my knee. The rain dimpled the mud puddles in the worn path that lead from the gardens to the trees, and there were earthworms among the roots now, stretching themselves in the moist soil. I pointed at two women who were still working among the flowers, in the rain. "Those women are funny."

"Why funny?" she asked.

"Because they wear those old-fashioned kerchiefs on their head. They look so bundled and roly-poly."

"That is way they always look."

"It's just funny, that's all."

"You have no women like that in America?" I shook my head.

"I do not remember women from Yonkers," she said. "I was very young."

The rain had stopped but a plop hit my nose and she laughed. I helped her up: she carefully brushed the gravel and dust off her bottom with her hands before we left the shelter of the tree. We took a different route back because she wasn't going home. "I go to aerobics class. I try to lose weight of Wojtek."

"That's smart."

We walked together, smiling. Wojtek was asleep. "I have only five pounds to go."

"You look pretty good to me."

The trunks of the trees were dark from the rain. So was the red sand in the park paths. The wheels of the baby carriage dug into it and made a grinding sound as she pushed. Large drops were still falling from some of the branches and leaves above us, and, when we reached the avenue where we had to part, I told her I'd call. "We can go to a movie."

"If projectionist does not die," she said. I laughed, but she was serious. "I never go to movies anymore. It is not easy, raising Wojtek on my own. I never have time to go out. I am young."

As I waited for the light to change cars passed by, their wheels throwing a fine spray off the asphalt. She crossed the street with a frown on her face, a married woman in dark sunglasses, pushing a baby to her aerobics class.

– – –

Before Warsaw, we had been traveling for two weeks with Eurrail passes. Tomasz was leading me around and I never knew which language I wasn't going to be able to speak next. I learned how to say "I don't know" in every one of them. I stared out the window in breaks from reading, at fields, at dogs, at a girl on a bicycle, with a sweater on her shoulders, knotted around her neck, waiting with one foot on the pedal for the train to pass. Hi who are you? I wanted to shout. I read *Men Without Women*. Outside Grenoble, at a red-roofed station, two girls chatted through the windows: one staying, the other on some unknown and untranslated adventure. I stood at the window, smoking pensively and trying to look handsome. Meanwhile, someone stole my camera.

– – –

From Berlin to Warsaw was little different. In the middle of the night, crossing the plains and forests of Western Poland in the dark, a band of light from the car windows paralleled the tracks: over grasses, the wall of a house, a stack of railroad ties. I wondered whose house it was. Were they asleep? Were they happy? Who stacked those railroad ties there? Everyone on the train seemed miserable. There was no room to lie down and my eyes were sore from lack of sleep. A man in a business suit was trying to sleep standing up, leaning his forehead against the wall. A boy sat at my feet, on the floor of the aisle, doing a crossword puzzle in Polish: all Z's, C's, and S's.

We arrived in Warsaw at dawn. The station had high ceilings, very boxy and Bauhaus. The walls were glass and let in gray shafts of light, and dozens of pigeons flew to roosts at the top of the windows, inside the building. Their feathers floated through the bands of light, the heavy sound of the beating wings audible above the murmur of the crowd. The waiting benches were spattered with dung. It was raining outside, streaking the windows and blurring the view. In the men's room, I waited in line behind a man who washed his neck with soap and steaming water. A kerchiefed woman selling squares of toilet paper stood next to me when I tried to urinate. I had stage fright. She had swollen ankles. No one else seemed to mind her presence. They sighed, leaning into the white porcelain urinals.

We drank vodka for breakfast with Tomasz's friends. One of them, Janusz, compulsively blinked. He kept blinking and talking and every time he said something everyone would laugh except me, because he was speaking Polish. He didn't know much English. When we were alone he pointed out the window at the rain and said, "Focking weather."

"He's hilarious," Tomasz told me, "but it's too hard to translate."

Tomasz talked to Janusz and pointed at me. Janusz smiled, blinked both his eyes, and said something, nodding his head enthusiastically. Tomasz laughed.

"I told him I want to get you a woman and he says he knows where some are, good Polish whores you can have for three hundred zloty."

Three hundred zloty was about fifty cents American. "No thanks," I said.

This was 1984, two years after martial law. Tadek promised to take me sightseeing in Warsaw but instead we went to the hard currency shop and bought vodka and cigarettes with American dollars, then spent the rest of the day drinking.

"I thought we were going to see the monument to the Warsaw Uprising?"

"Is big monument in park," he said. "Drink."

—   —   —

The week after our meeting I purposely didn't call Helena, even though I had nothing to do. In the mornings I stared out the window at children playing in the street, an old woman tossing bread to pigeons in front of the building, and the long queues at kiosks. I tried to understand the city. Everyone spoke of martial law and Lech Walesa. The symbol for Solidarity looked like a large S with a ship's anchor superimposed upon it. These were everywhere: in the elevators, in the bathrooms, along brick walls.

Tadek the alcoholic talked about Helena over breakfast, his mustache filled with crumbs.

"She asked about you," he said. "She likes you."

"But she's married. I don't want to be a home wrecker." Tadek shook his head as if this didn't matter. His eyes seemed to droop even further than usual. He smiled and said, "There is saying in Poland: you can take a man's money, you can take a man's woman," he paused, and held up one finger. "Just don't touch his vodka."

One afternoon Tadek and Janusz asked if I liked sightseeing and if I had seen everything I had wanted to.

"Well, I would like to go to Treblinka."

"Treblinka?" They looked at each other. Janusz blinked and nodded. Tadek started coughing, he laughed so hard. "We can go to Treblinka, yes, we can do that," he said. "But no one has car."

"How far is it from Warsaw?"

"Not far."

"Then let's take a taxi."

"A taxi to Treblinka," said Tadek. "That's bloody great. That's smashing." He wiped tears of laughter from his eyes. "And let's take pictures of ourselves in front of the showers with your Japanese camera."

Tadek put a bottle of vodka in his coat and we convinced a taxi driver to take us there, who was surly at first, but after much talk from blinking Janusz and drinking Tadek he agreed, laughing. They talked the entire time with the driver, who had been a little boy living in Warsaw during World War Two. Now and then Tadek translated something. "He says the difference between Poland and America is the difference between Treblinka and Disneyland."

Janusz had fallen asleep by the time we reached Treblinka. Most of the buildings were gone and there was a wooden sign up commemorating the holocaust and the history of the concentration camp. There was a field of white stone markers. All around us were pine and spruce trees and the forest looked like a state park in Wisconsin. There were cows in the field across from us, and crows cawing and flapping their wings, then coasting, then flapping again, black shapes against a white sky. Tadek walked around with me, drinking from the bottle of vodka. It was raining, as always. The taxi driver didn't get out of his car. I took a picture of the sign but didn't ask Tadek to pose. We were shivering by the time we got back in the car.

That night, empty bottles of vodka sat on the small table in our living room like bowling pins. We drank cold vodka and toasted "Na zdrowie!" The air was blue and thick with cigarette smoke. Tadek arrived with Helena. I smiled shyly, and guiltily, as Tadek sat her down on the couch next to me and said, "I brought both of you present." Helena slapped him on the arm and asked me for a cigarette.

"Maybe you have something to drink? Why did you never call?"

"I wanted to. But you're married."

She shook her head and smiled at me. "I heard about your sightseeing."

"It was nothing. I've still been lonely."

"You have?"

"Uh huh. I cry myself to sleep at night. The neighbors complain. They bang on the walls."

She smiled. "I cry also. I have to change . . . what do you call them? Thing you put on pillows, each night, because they are so wet from tears."

"Maybe we should cry together."

Helena squeezed my hand and we were quiet for a moment. I rubbed my thumb against her palm. The others played cards, with the only lamp in the apartment in the middle of the card table; where we sat, it was dark enough for me to put my hand inside the back of her blouse, feeling her spine, working my fingers into the waist of her pants.

"I cannot stay here long," she said. "Grzegorz is taking care of my baby and he will not know what to do if Wojtek wets his diapers. I have to leave."

"Can you come back?'

"Come with me? Please? I will put Wojtek to sleep. Then we talk."

She walked out into the hall as I told Tadek where I was going. Janusz winked.

Finally it had stopped raining, although large puddles still stood in the road and on the sidewalks. We reached a taxi stand. Helena waved her hand but none of the cars stopped. "In movies," she said, "in Polish movies, as soon as people walk out onto street and raise their hand, taxi pulls up. But in real life, you have to wait for hours."

The streetlights stood in a brilliant line along the avenue, circled by haloes filled with moths. Helena put a bobby pin in her soft brown hair to keep it off her neck. "What are you thinking?" she said. "You never say anything. I never know what you are thinking."

"Neither do I."

"Yes you do. You will not tell me."

"I think I feel strange."

She put both hands up to rearrange the back of her hair and nodded, pulling the bobby pin out and placing it in a better location. "So do I, but that is fun, right?"

At her building she put me in her friend Katja's apartment, the one where the party had been, before she went upstairs to the apartment she shared with her mother to put her baby to sleep and let Grzegorz go home. Grzegorz was a good friend—one of the men at the party who had wanted to beat up Tomasz. She said he only talked tough, but was really very nice. Later that night, after Tomasz and I had left, he had gotten into a fight with her husband and had knocked her husband's teeth out, then the next morning had paid to get them replaced. "This happens many times," she said. "They are friends."

Katja had brought back oranges from Berlin, which were impossible to get in Warsaw unless you were a member of the Communist Party. They were on the table in the living room, probably twenty pounds, most of them green and lopsided with mold.

"Do you eat these?" I asked.

"What? They are rotten. You think us animals."

"No . . . but, I mean, what are they doing here?"

"For juice."

The phone rang and she said, "That is my mother." Her baby was crying and she had to go up and put him to sleep. It was after midnight by now. "Do not leave," she said. "Stay here and I will call. When mother goes to sleep you can come."

I sat in the apartment for a few minutes alone, staring at the rotten oranges. The phone rang and it was Katja, speaking Polish.

"Nie mowi Popolsku," I said. "Ja jestem Americanin." She kept asking the same question. I heard her say Helena's name but could only repeat my Berlitz phrases. "Dziekuje bardzo," I said, and hung up. (Thank you very much.)

Helena walked in, holding back a slobbering Rotweiler. "This is Caspar Weinburger," she said. The dog sniffed me and shook his stumpy tail. "Let us go upstairs, but we have to be very quiet. I brought Caspar so he would smell you and not bark."

She put her finger to my lips as she opened the door and stood in the hallway, pointing to a small door on the right, which had a foggy pane of glass in the middle. The only light in the room was a small lamp with a towel thrown over it. I could barely see little Wojtek asleep in his cradle. The room was narrow, straight, and at the end of it, beside a window with blue curtains, was a single bed. The floor was cluttered with toys and baby things, barely enough room to walk. We sat down quietly and Helena opened the windows behind the curtains, lit a cigarette, and handed me a plastic cup full of vodka. She blew the smoke out the window and I could tell she was listening to the other room. "Can you hear that?" she whispered, taking my hand in hers. Very faintly I heard something that sounded like muttering. "It is my mother. She talks to herself in her sleep. It is good sign. When she is not talking to herself I cannot tell whether she is asleep or not." After she told me what the sound was I understood and listened to it.

"Are you scared?"

"A little."

"Feel." She took my hand and placed it on her chest. Her heart was beating beneath the skin, and I could see the veins in her neck pulsing. She closed her eyes and held my hand there. "You are breaking my heart."

— — —

The first trams of the morning had begun running when I left, the arched connecting cables on their roofs throwing off sparks against the overhead wires, whining. The sky was filled with the pale blue light of a cloudy dawn. It was cold and the clothes I wore from the night before were thin and damp. I shivered, walking with my hands in my pockets through the wet grass of the courtyard to the tram stop she had directed me to. The dew stained the tips of my shoes dark. The avenue I skirted along had no sidewalks and I had to sidestep the puddles. At the border of one of them, a crow was crushed into the mud, its jaws gaping open, the black feathers criss-crossed by the muddy treadmarks of bicycle tires.

— — —

Helena and I made love again the next night, very quietly, muffling ourselves, listening to her mother talk in her sleep through the thin walls. Helena turned her face away when I tried to kiss her, and put her finger on my lips. "Why won't you kiss me?" I whispered.

"My husband tastes always of vodka. Is disgusting."

Her breasts were small, her hips narrow, and beside her, I felt thick and clumsy. The striped shadows from Wojtek's crib crossed her pillow as she bit her lip, turning her head back and forth as I moved slowly and silently inside her. When Wojtek started crying she told me not to stop and, keeping her eyes closed and locking her calves against the backs of my knees, she reached out with one hand to rock Wojtek's cradle, opening her legs wider, matching the cradle's rhythm with our motion.

"You seem like person from another planet," she said afterwards, her cheek against my chest. "Like person from moon."

I invited her to a wedding reception I had to go to, but she couldn't leave her house because there was no one to take care of Wojtek. That night, she asked if I danced with other girls and was jealous. She wanted to know who they were and what they looked like. Did I like dancing with them? She was a very good dancer if I would just let her show me. She cried while we made love and said she couldn't stand the thought of my leaving. What would she do after I was gone?

"Maybe you stay?" she asked. "You could teach English. Everyone wants to learn. They want to know American."

–  –  –

Tomasz took me away for the weekend, kayaking in the lake district north of Warsaw. He borrowed an uncle's Polish Fiat and we drove past plowed fields and churches, and horse-drawn wagons in the road.

"I couldn't just . . . stay here . . . could I?" I asked.

"Sure. The question is, do you want to?"

Tadek passed back a bottle of vodka, wiping the mouth on his sleeve. "Is no money in Warsaw. After six months, you go hungry."

"I could get by."

"You're crazy," said Tomasz. "You're insane."

The lake district was a soft landscape full of low rolling hills, fields of wheat, wooden bridges, and swans. We rented heavy wooden kayaks and paddled them in dark, cold water. I paddled with blinking Janusz and our oars kept knocking against each other, and I shivered from the water that splashed back onto me. In the shallows the mud oozed between our toes and we had to watch for broken bottles of vodka close to the pier. We rented cabins that smelled of cedar and played poker by lantern light. The shore of the lake was serene and silent at dusk, except for the sounds of frogs and fish breaking the surface. A storm came in one afternoon and while we were out and we were soaked by the time we reached the pier. The wind roughed the lake into white-capped waves. We dried out with towels and built a fire in the fireplace. I imagined vacationing here, with Helena. We would make love in the cabin, paddle among the cattails, with the swans, her fine hair glowing like a halo with the sun behind her, her eyes closed, waiting for my touch.

That night we had a dinner of vodka, a round loaf of stale bread, and white cheese wrapped in wax paper. I was getting used to eating like that, and enjoyed sawing off hunks of the cheese with my Swiss Army knife. I told Tomasz, "I could get used to this. I could be happy here."

"You're not serious, are you?"

"Well . . . ."

"You can't stay here. You'd make me feel guilty."

"You're the one who wanted me to come in the first place."

"But I didn't think you'd enlist in the Polish army."

"I didn't expect it to be like this."

Tomasz poured us two more drinks. "Think about Paris," he said, winking. "Think about Norwegian girls."

— — —

The night we returned to Warsaw there was a going-away party; all of Tomasz's friends showed up and we drank too much vodka. I didn't call Helena. I told myself there was no time. No one took my idea to stay in Warsaw seriously.

"You are lucky," said Tadek. "You can go or stay. You are lucky son of bitch."

The next morning, while Tomasz packed, I went to call Helena. An old woman was selling flowers across from the phone booth, and I bought a bunch of purple tulips, whose roots were still tangled with soil, for Helena, putting my money in the wrinkled palm of the old woman, who worked her jaw as she counted it, as if chewing something. Helena's voice was meek.

"You will not stay?" she asked.

"Well . . ." I waited, I don't know, for something. For her to beg, to get mad, to hate me. The window in the phone booth was cracked. Finally, "I guess not."

Tomasz and I arrived at the train station early, our backpacks full of vodka and chocolate. At the cafeteria I couldn't eat, sitting across from a man with a huge wart between his eyes.

We moved our packs to the platform and I went back to wait for Helena. I had my camera out and the flash attached to it, but when she arrived, smiling, wearing the same Snoopy sweatshirt she wore the day we walked in the park, she made me swear not to take her picture.

"I am not trophy," she said. "Something you hang on wall."

"I know that."

She gave me a book of etchings by Polish artists, and I gave her the flowers. It came time to board the train. We walked a few feet away from the others; too many things were happening at once. I couldn't concentrate. Janusz had arrived to see us off. We were headed for Norway, to pick strawberries and make some money. Janusz said he might meet up with us, he could hitchhike through Sweden, after taking the ferry to Malmo, but he wasn't sure. Tadek nodded and said, "I know what you mean. Like your Mr. T. S. Eliot says, Should I part my hair behind? Do I dare eat a peach?"

Helena squeezed my hand. "I cannot believe you are leaving. In minute you will be on train and we will never see again."

She started crying after we kissed; the train lurched; I grabbed my backpack and hopped aboard. I pulled down the window and held her hand as, almost imperceptibly at first, the train began to move, quietly and smoothly. I said "Na razie," a phrase she had taught me. It meant "See you later." The purple of the tulips seemed to swirl in the air with her blue eyes and trembling lower lip, against the gray background of the train station, the shiny black boots of Polish soldiers, her brown hair, all blurred by the smooth movement of the wheels slowly turning, gaining speed. Helena reminded me of Anna Karenina waiting for the cars to pass before throwing herself under the wheels of the train, and, overwhelmed, I missed the exact moment her fingers slipped away. She stood there on the platform, hands cupped over her mouth, watching me leave. I leaned out and, in the windows of the motionless train across the tracks, caught a reflection of myself, waving.

# This Whatever We Have

It was the kind of day the kind of moment the kind of embarrassing incident that you later wish you could take back you wince groan kick yourself ask stupidly what was I thinking? But the moment occurred, someone saw something—not that those allegations could not be denied. There were no actual records of it—if there were, I'd use the paper shredder. I have one in my office. I don't really need it. I think it's cool. It gives me that 007 savoir faire, like an insider with secrets to hide. Think *espionage*. Think *Mission Impossible*. Think self-destruction.

But this is hardly the Pentagon. In my office, the paper shredder—a shiny metal box with blades, like a prop from Terry Gilliam's *Brazil*—is mainly art. (The *idea* of destruction. The *idea* of rewriting history.) Plus, it serves as a recycling tool. We must keep things tidy in my world, which is an office on the eighteenth floor, a nice view of midtown from one window, Japanese comic book posters on my walls, a light box for viewing slides, my cluttered, glass-topped desk, modeling agency black books neatly shelved. I'm the brains behind people selling things. My job is seduction. But there are limits. And on the day I crossed them, Elke had the tips of my fingers in her mouth—well, just inside her mouth, lipstick glazing my fingerprints—when June walked in and dropped everything, stopped everything, threw a monkey wrench in the middle of my struggling career.

"Pardon me," she said. She glanced about, scanning the room, searching for a handy subtext, for neutering scissors, an excuse for living. In her distraction, I wiped a pink streak of lipstick on the white cotton of my cuff.

"Maybe I caught you at a bad time," said June. She lifted the file folders in her hands, like a bailiff with today's docket. "I've got mock-ups for you to look at, but it's okay. I'll come back."

Elke squirmed her shoulders, shifting her blouse into place. "That's a good idea," I said.

"Better yet, when you're ready, give me a ring."

"I could do that." I touched my face for no reason whatsoever. "We were just going over some things that needed attention."

June smiled. "I'm not your mother."

I said, "I never thought you were."

Elke was sitting on my desktop, her pumps resting on the drafting table behind me, her back to the door and to June. After that slight adjustment, she did not move. She did not flinch. She did not reach to button her blouse. It had a wide, soft collar, pearl buttons, silk fabric of the deepest blue, that when the halogen light shone on its edges, shimmered to purple. It was untucked and unbuttoned, and undone was the clasp of her it's-a-girl pink French 34C cups. Without turning to look at June, she asked, "Is it raining again? Tell me it isn't. Tell me it's sunny."

June pretended for one moment that Elke did not exist. There is hate and there is envy, and then there is a cloudy, viscous, rancid mixture of the two. Elke was famous around the office for being the new boss's illusive object of desire. June was famous around the office for having mistakenly, drunkenly confessed that it had been six years since the last time she had experienced what some call sexual intercourse, telling this to Shelly Curapada the Big Mouth. June's lips were coated with sneer and disgust as she took two steps backward, crossed the threshold, and paused before closing the door.

"Open or shut?"

"Shut."

She closed it slowly, as if the room were wired to blow. That simple movement took approximately ten minutes. Finally, the tongue of the lock clucked gently, the sound you hear while trying to walk a straight line down the halls when returning red-nosed and wobbly from a two-hour, four-gimlet lunch.

Elke pushed her Jerry Hall hair out of her face and blinked as if she were being blinded by the flashes of paparazzi. "That woman is a menace," she said. "If there is any justice in the world, any at all, her car will die on the FDR tonight." She narrowed her eyes. "Is sabotage a crime?"

I leaned over my desk, put my forehead against the documents of neglect there, and started to pound, once for every word. "We. Are. Now. Totally. Fucked."

When I looked up, Elke was buttoning her beauty back into place. The tiny cupid tattoo above her left breast said buh-bye as I saw my career flash before my eyes, the way the drowning are said to review home-movie highlights of all those swirling years. In recent months, mine were all lowlights: the wacky toothpaste commercial in which the woman's smile so dazzles her boss she gets the big promotion, cued by the catchphrase, *Teeth this white can't be beat!* Or the Chevrolet campaign with a Lumina carefully circling a crater on the moon, voiceover saying, *Lumina—It's positively lunar!* I hadn't had a pitch that was used in nine months. I'd lost the touch. I'd hit a lull. A dry spell. Or, as someone had said about June's revelation of six years without sex: "That's not just a dry spell. That's, like, Ethiopia."

Elke saw the panicky look on my face and scrunched her mouth—a twist down and to the left—to signal wrong-reaction-in-progress. "Don't be the Drama King."

I told her that I wasn't. I wasn't paranoid. But this was Trouble. I said, "You know what this means, don't you?" Even sitting down, I felt weak. Like I was donating blood by accident.

Elke stood, smoothed her miniskirt, and ruffled my hair. "Have tongue will wag? So what. Besides, it might be to your advantage. It will throw the dogs off your trail."

"Since when did I become the hunted?"

"Everyone thinks you're doing Mia."

This was news to me. For months now Mia and I had been obsessive-compulsive for each other, but I didn't know it was so obvious. I said, "But she's lesbian."

Elke gave me a we're-not-that-stupid look. "With her I think that's a good faith agreement, not a binding contract."

"With me it's more like Double Indemnity."

Elke shook her head, her hair swaying, loopy as a grass skirt of harvest wheat. She was raised in Hawaii, the daughter of a rich divorce lawyer. Think questionable moral fiber. Think luau. Think the TV commercial: *How 'bout a nice Hawaiian Punch?* "Get a grip," she said. "Remember the words of Mr. Wilde. The only thing worse."

I sighed and began to rearrange the seventeen felt tip pens on my desk top. "No. That's not true. There is something worse. It's called Unemployment."

Elke rolled her eyes, rolled her hips, rolled back the welcome mat for yours truly. She lifted a clear plastic sheet of 35 mm slides off my desk and swatted me with it. "Now I know you're overreacting."

She sashayed to the door and paused before touching the knob, looking back without anger, without fear, with years of good luck behind her and a certainty of the same ahead. "Cool is the way to be."

— — —

Cool was easy for Elke to say. She reigned as the No. 1 office ingénue. An ex-fashion model who came on like Miss Innocent in a cute meet, but once you got to know her, evolved into a daily edition of bad news. She pranced about the office to the tune of "I Can't Help It I'm Beautiful!" She'd already been the black widow for one poor shmuck. If not for this, she probably would have put the sting on me. But I wasn't having it. I saw her riding in that self-obsession parade, sitting high in the limousine, waving, tossing candy to the crowd. She saw others only in relation to what they could do for her, how they could shower her with attention, how they could adore her, tell her she was beautiful, offer the adulation she certainly deserved now didn't she? My design assistant and No. 1 forbidden love, Mia, agreed with my take on Elke, finding her fascinating and repulsive at the same time.

We made up story boards for a TV sitcom titled *All About Elke!* With a cartoon gorgeous girl figure—half-*That Girl* and half-Barbie doll—prancing before a backdrop of island huts on fire, we'd have a Phil Hartman voiceover saying, "There may be CIA operatives waterskiing in Puerto Rico, but it's *All About Elke!*" Cut to image of barbie-doll Elke with matching outfits and accessories, prancing before a high-drama EMS scene, à la the true crime TV shows, the voiceover saying, "There may be an eight-year-old trapped in an abandoned mine shaft, but it's *All About Elke!*" Follow with an image of a hydrogen bomb mushroom cloud, and the Elke character refusing her gas mask, sassing, "I don't think so!" as the voiceover says, "The world may be trembling on the brink of nuclear holocaust, but it's *All About Elke!*"

We were not having an affair. I knew better. Yes, the flesh is weak. But my fingers in her mouth, her blouse unbuttoned, that was just a game, that was *All About Elke*.

It started when she E-mailed me that she had some juicy dirt to make my day. After lunch she popped by my office to chat. This was right before June caught us in her net of envy. (Caught Elke trying to wrap me around her little fingers.) This was the dirt: She told me that, the day before, our new boss, Chevron Cameron, had come on to her in his office.

What did she mean, come on? I wanted dirt. Were we talking a proposition? Were we talking sexual harassment? "What exactly did he say?"

"Wouldn't you like to know." She scooted her rump onto my desk and took the pen out of my hands. Her legs, sheathed in pantyhose, were endless and otherworldly. I told her she should be careful, and she just gave me a stupid-you look, tucking the pen behind one ear. "You really want to know?" she asked.

"Sure."

"He said he'd like to see me naked."

I shrugged. Cameron had a way of getting to the point. I said, "He's not the only one."

Elke smiled with the innocence of a hardcore website, and arched an eyebrow. "Oh, really?"

"Really."

That's when she began unbuttoning her deepest blue silk blouse till she reached the pink lace of her C-cups, watching me sip a nervous cup of titillation and dread. Leaning forward, she squirmed half-free of her sleeves, revealing more tanning-spa skin than I should see, and said, "Don't you hate that word? Bra? I do."

I pointed my right index finger at her like the barrel of a gun. "You are trouble." She made a pouty face, and the crisp edge of my resolve softened like milk chocolate in a warm pocket. *Melts in your mouth, not in your hands!* She looked through the clouds of my willpower, catching a glimpse of my murky and unredeemable soul. "But you love trouble, don't you?" she asked. We were plunging earthward, but I was the only one who lacked a chute; my bones would shatter, but Elke would land like a feather boa.

I knew what was happening: I was the guest star in this week's episode of *All About Elke*. In the inappropriate glow of the office lamps, she floated above me like a Madison Avenue angel, like a sexy ad for chocolate or liquor. The air around her was all Obsession. I felt like the victim of one of those surprise-birthday-party pranks, as if I'd been blindfolded, taken up in a small plane, and pushed out the door to try the thrill of skydiving. As in an out-of-body experience, I watched as she reached out and took my pointing hand, pulled it to her mouth, and began to lick my fingers.

That's when June opened the door.

—  —  —

I moved through the rest of the day like a deep sea diver in giant squid territory, like a poet in Stalingrad, circa 1937. Like a fad on the way out. The office cleared after six, and Mia, who could tell something was up, invited me over for drinks. She was my wildest lover and female best friend, famous for being a lipstick lesbian, which provided a nice smokescreen for that Robert Palmer way I thought of her—Simply Irresistible. She was all about contradictions. Mix and match. Black leather jacket and junior-high I.D. bracelets. She read Mark Leyner and listened to Ella Fitzgerald. She had a thin silver nose ring, but wore her hair in a good-girl French braid.

Sipping martinis, she listened to my whole story, eyes going wide when I reached the finger-sucking demonstration and June's dramatic entrance. But she didn't think it was that big of a deal, certainly not like I did, like The Beginning of the End.

"Poor baby." She pooched out her lips, making a pouty face, and brushed the hair off my forehead. She advised me to calm down and not overreact. I had a tendency to do that, she noted. "Get a haircut. It'll make you feel like a new man."

"Cameron will can me if he thinks I'm after Elke."

She didn't think so. The world wasn't as bad as all that. Good will prevail. To stop me from stressing out, she offered a hug, pulling me from my chair by my hands and wrapping me close. The warmth of her body was an aura, a glow that emanated from her clothes, and I lingered there, wrapped in the cocoon of someone I could trust, someone who knew the shape of my scars and still loved me.

Talking into my shoulder, she said, "There's more to this than you think. June knows there's something going on between us, and she's jealous. So she's trying to use this thing with Elke against you."

"She makes my scrotum shrivel."

Mia laughed. "Don't you worry. If she so much as hurts a hair on your body, I'll scratch out her eyeballs."

In the silence that followed, we held each other tight, until I pulled back from her and lifted her chin to look into her eyes, "Really?"

"Yes, really. Isn't it really obvious? You really aren't that bright, are you?"

I smiled at her and said, "I'm really not. But I'd really like to kiss you."

She stared at my mouth and asked if I remembered the recent Nike shoe campaign.

"Just do it?"

In the dizzy spell of her eyelashes, we began to kiss. I couldn't stop. She finally turned her mouth away and whispered wait, stop for a moment, her toes were itching.

"Your toes?"

She nodded, flushed and dizzy and vulnerable. "When I want to make love to someone, someone important to me, my toes itch."

I didn't know what to say, but she added that it was a good sign. Her toes only itched for the best people. She started walking backwards, toward the stairs, toward her bedroom. "My toes are never wrong."

— — —

The next day, my One Hope—Richard Boone, chief officer in charge of consumer brainwashing and one of the best—took me to lunch. When we ordered drinks, and when they arrived, he gave me the longest look, flipped his napkin into his lap like a miniature picnic tablecloth, and generally assumed the role of the gay uncle I never had but always yearned for. He said, "What . . . ." He paused and looked around the Italian place, as if scanning for corporate spies. "What do you honestly think we are going to do with you?"

"We," I started to say . . . then stopped. Who is this *we*? We are salaried types. We don't get paid by the hour. We do our jobs. We do them well. We're good at them. So we make a mistake now and then. So we got caught sexing around on our down time? Is that a sin? It was a Tuesday afternoon and there was nothing better to do. We stay late, we work weekends, we fucking *live* at the office. We eat there. We fight, break-up, make-up, yearn and frustrate there. Sometimes we even sleep there. If you ask me, we might as well fuck there. Is that a crime? Tell me. Show me the clause in my contract.

Still. Love is one thing. Company policy is another. "We . . ." I said, "are waiting for the ax to fall."

Richard frowned at this poor excuse for the power of positive thinking. "Don't go throwing a pity party. What's that? Your first taste of breaking a sexual taboo? Join the club."

I agreed with him, admitting he was right, that I shouldn't overreact.

"The first step in solving any difficult situation is identifying the problem. Do you know what yours is?"

"Elke works under me."

Rick made a questioning face. "I figured her to be the one on top."

"Would you stop?"

"Touchy touchy." Rick stared at his drink as if there were a feminine hygiene product in it. "Did they put any vodka in this? This looks like one of those restaurants where they've substituted Folger's Instant for the real thing and no one complains when they come to the table with a video camera to ask their reaction." He had the waiter bring us two more, doubles this time, and in the lull between drinks, explained, with the patience reserved for the slow-minded, that my behavior could be perceived as taking advantage of my position of power. Not to mention said love thing was the boss's Dream Girl USA.

"I know. You're not telling me anything new here. I need Insight."

"For your benefit, I think it would be a good thing for us to review the Sexual Harassment Policy handout." He took a personnel brochure from his coat pocket and unfolded it. "Shall we?"

As he scanned it, I told him it wasn't necessary. Nothing was going on between me and Elke.

"What about Mia?" He gave me a you-can't-fool-me look. "That girl is cuckoo for your cocoa puffs."

I insisted that she wasn't, but he only nodded and said, "Uh huh." I asked him what was so wrong with that, anyway? Show me the line where it's forbidden. We're consenting adults!

He said, "It's a question of how that consent is obtained."

Truth was, I hadn't read the sexual harassment policy statement. Yadda Yadda Yadda. I skipped it. I didn't want to know. After a moment, I admitted all of that. I told him, "I'm a busy man, you know. I had something pressing. Better things to do."

"What?" he asked. "Consensual digitilingus?" He held his finger in the air to catch the waiter's attention.

"That's not a crime," I said. "That's only Incriminating."

He smiled like I'm-On-Your-Side, Pal. "You don't have to tell me. Save it for the deposition." The waiter arrived and Richard ordered another martini for himself, and pointing at me, he said, "And bring him another. What's that you're drinking? A Long Island Lolita?"

— — —

To get my mind off Looming Doom, I plunged into work. It was my mission impossible to come up with a new slogan for the Montenegro print, radio and TV ads. We had a huge budget. Money no object. Not when you're in the brainwashing department. We pay for this, of course. All of us. We pay millions to have idiotic jingles planted in our brains. Just do it! Just say no! Does it make us happy? Where's the beef? Don't ask. Do your job. I holed up in my office, door closed and locked, and brainstormed. Avoiding everyone, even Mia, I snuck out later and went home. Coffee was the key. A good cup of joe. Requiem for a java junkie. I needed concepts:

Coffee, not love, is what makes the world goes round.

What if there were no coffee? We'd get less done.

(We'd get some goddamned sleep. I would kill for that. I would kill for sleep. Wrong track.)

Ask not what you can do for your coffee, ask what your coffee can do for you.

Testimonials would be the key: Picture a worn-out fortysomething average guy with loosened tie and a briefcase: "I want a cup of coffee that will brighten my day."

That seemed the best idea I could come up with, and after jotting down a list of possible slogans, I took a break. From the balcony of my Riverside Drive apartment, I checked out the world across the Hudson. The skies were clear over Jersey. Air traffic coming into

Newark International was heavy as always. The jets were beautiful lights drifting through the blue-black sky, twenty or thirty of them in motion at a time. Beyond its beauty, there was the hint of disaster. It could have been an evacuation. Hearts in throats. A rush for the gates. "You don't understand! We have to make that flight! It's our only hope!" I'd sworn to myself not to have more than two drinks a night and felt the ice of number four clink against my teeth. It reminded me how, when I got home, my answering machine was blinking like the navigation lights of a Virgin airlines commuter jet. I had three messages. Richard asked, "Where were you all afternoon? Did you fall off the world? Don't start slinking around now, acting guilty." Someone from my alma mater called, requesting money. And there was Mia: "I miss you. I need you. Meow meow."

— — —

Next day at the office the hallways were filled with a threatening buzz. Voices softened when I passed by, conversations hushed; in this mood of muffled rumor, the most ordinary sounds—the click of a briefcase lock, the whirr of a hard drive, the coughs of now-suspicious colleagues—scored the skin of my brain like papercuts. At coffee break, June trailed me to the corner deli and confirmed that my small world was getting smaller.

"Are you okay?" she asked, a total lack of concern in her voice. "You're not looking very well."

I shrugged. "Couldn't sleep."

Her eyes registered joy but her lips said, "You should take something for that."

"I do."

I take a lot of pills. I take pills at night to fall asleep. I never sleep. Pills help, though. I take everything. Lightweight stuff like Tylenol PM, which gives me woolly dreams right after sex, right as the PM part kicks in and I'm falling asleep, the smell of Mia's juices on my lips, my fingernails, under my fingernails, in the curls of my hair. The nightmares: I'm in an underground parking garage, trying to find a place to have sex with Mia, there are soldiers searching for us, I'm carrying this huge weapon that looks like the cross between a pike and a snow shovel; it's completely dark and I stumble through the concrete murk, Mia covering my back . . . . I take Xanax, which gives me a wonderful drowsiness and makes for easy sex and a quick light's out. I take Darvocet and talk in my sleep about Chinese girls in sequined gowns and I take Melatonin when no one's in bed with me.

Not long ago Mia snagged some pharmaceutical morphine, and we couldn't keep our hands off each other. They were delicious green pills. We didn't know what to expect but what the hell, you only live once. We put a movie on, but became quickly distracted, kissing and rubbing each other, sweetly describing how much we loved each other, slipping our tongues over our mouths like they were the lips between her legs. In the middle of watching a bad Hollywood witty hit-man movie, 2 *Valleys in a Day*, I think it was, she shimmied out of her jeans, opened her legs, and I curled into her like a comma with a vigorous tongue, lapping happily at her lollipop, as she grinned ecstatically at the video we both never finished watching.

But I couldn't mention this to June. She would not approve. She would note how I had supported Mia's last promotion. Is it sexual harassment yet?

She stood behind me in line just to make me miserable, tapping the counter with her pepper-mace key ring. I ordered a double latte and offered to buy her one, but she shook her head.

"I can't take caffeine. It makes me nervous."

June is a classic case of short woman's complex, a Napoleon

Bonapartette. She's short and fat and hyper-everything. She approaches life as punishment, not reward. Her hair is cut severely and her glasses have squarish black frames. She sees me as a threat. I'm having too good of a time. Life should be miserable. She's been on antidepressants for years now and they don't help. Nothing helps. She's miserable and resents the fact that the rest of the world isn't. She's chock full of Zoloft and if you licked her neck, the skin would taste bitter as bad aspirin. She told Shelly Curapada that she thinks her father molested her as a child. She doesn't remember it. In truth, her father is a kind and now-discouraged man, but that means squat. She's sure the lurid memory is repressed.

What else would cause this angst? Maybe it was Uncle Marvin? Cousin Wagner? The problem is men. They only want one thing you know. And that Elke. She gives the rest of us a bad name. She's fucking her way to the top, is what she is. Doesn't she have any self-respect? Doesn't she know it's not fair? We can't all be beautiful. We can't all be talented. We can't all be smart. Most of us aren't. What about us? Huh? What about the miserable of the world? There are rules prohibiting this kind of behavior. There are laws. She can't get away with this. *The time for misery is now.*

On the elevator, June asked if I had a minute to talk something over.

"Well, I am kind of busy."

"It shouldn't take long."

Her office was decorated in a Drab World scheme. She asked how my coffee campaign was progressing.

"Just fine, thank you."

"It's hard to do something new with commodities, isn't it?"

"We try. Is there something in particular . . . ?"

She kept her focus dead on me. "It's a rather delicate matter. It's just that I think we may have some trouble with Elke." She blinked for a moment, giving me pause to flinch. When I didn't offer anything, she said, "We've already had one law suit. I don't think another is necessary, is it?"

"I hope not."

She held a pencil in her hands, and for a moment, as it felt the pressure, it stood in as the metaphorical equivalent of my neck, under threat of snapping. "I just wanted to warn you. It would be most unpleasant if she filed charges."

"Well." I stood up. I didn't know what to do with my hands, so I brushed the disgust off my slacks. "I think that's my phone ringing."

— — —

After that, I huddled in my office with a cup of latte and a quart of rage. Even cottontails, when backed into a corner, turn ferocious. I felt very much the white male tired of taking his licks. I wanted to stand at a podium before millions and defend myself. Be like Peter Finch in *Network*, shout, "I'm mad as hell and I'm not going to take it anymore!" Declare my firm belief in consensual sexual harassment. It's a good thing. If two people are willing to break the rules and risk everything just to pinch each other's nipples, or put their tongues in each other's ears, kiss till their lips are swollen—more power to 'em. It's a sign of courage. A sign of life. Defiance.

My ace card was that I sensed Chevron Cameron shared my convictions.

We might well be the convicted, and remain free.

Like, maybe, Henry David Thoreau with a hard-on.

Besides, June was assuming she had power to wield, and I sensed that might not be true in this new regime. June had been the favorite of our ex-boss, Morton Lieberman, who had recently been spirited away by a major cable network to help brainwash millions of very-much-suspecting and suspicious but nevertheless easily duped Americans. In his glory days, Morton would introduce June at staff meetings by saying, "Gentlemen, let's give a warm welcome to my pit bull."

His replacement, Chevron Cameron, was a wild card. He was a dead ringer for Donald Sutherland, and, like Alfred Hitchcock, wore the same suit every day. He was famous for ending conversations if not relationships by saying, "Enough. We'll talk later."

He was rumored by some to be a degenerate. But what—in this day and age of bestiality websites, teenage sexting, and *Mad About Threesomes* Marv Albert dressed in ladies scanties, biting and sodomizing "bad girls" who snatch his hairpiece in horror—does that mean? There were stories. He dated Jennifer Aniston before she became a Friend. He had a column of ex-girlfriend names tattooed on his back. He was glimpsed smoking opium with Jack Nicholson at his place on Martha's Vineyard, and he'd once been romantically (and perhaps physically) linked to Princess Di, the stock of this story rising after she reached the end of her road. All this was in the category of legend, not truth. The only thing certain: He preferred women over men. So do I.

In only his second week aboard, he caught me and Mia on the roof, a pipe in her hands and the incense wind of marijuana swirling about my face. For a heartbeat the three of us blinked and looked each other over like Lee Van Cleef, Eli Wallach, and Clint Eastwood in *The Good, the Bad, and the Ugly.* Then I offered him a taste.

He nodded and grinned. "Generosity is a virtue," he said, then ripped off a mean hit, sucking it deep into his lungs and not exhaling till he coughed. After the third hit I asked why he'd been looking for us. He seemed to be thinking for a moment, then grinned. "I forgot."

We all broke up laughing, our voices echoing down the stairs. When we returned to the office, he asked if his eyes were a knock-off. Mia graciously offered her Visine: *Gets the red out!* He inserted a few drops, blinked and wiped them away, smoothed his jacket, then left us, saying, "I think misbehavior is a good thing. It keeps the blood flowing. Carry on."

— — —

To vent my spleen, I came up with new slogans, fresh from the inspiration of June:

"I want a cup of coffee that will make mine enemies' crops wither on the vine. I want a cup of coffee that will spoil the food in their refrigerators, that will make their cars not start in the morning. I want a cup of coffee to make their body odor strong and their water pressure weak, so they'll never get the shampoo out and will be visited by a host of bad hair days."

— — —

Elke and I agreed to meet for lunch, to map a strategy on how to deal with this. Already I didn't trust her. She was acting funny about the whole thing. More than anything, she seemed amused. Even pleased. She liked to be the center of attention, the focus of the buzz.

In a Spanish restaurant specializing in tapas dishes, we met. I had chicken and she had not a care in the world. "Do you realize I can see the future?" She played with her hair as she spoke. "You don't believe me, do you?"

What's to believe? Time is linear. The future is what comes next. After lunch, Elke would say she was tired and could I make an excuse for her back at the office? She wanted to do some shopping. Later I would go home to my bachelor's apartment with my electric sockets and cable TV staring back at me. I shrugged. "You're not Cassandra, are you?"

"Who's that? One of your many exes?"

I smiled as if Snow White had just stepped on my foot, thinking how my life had been played out in restaurants. Truth is, there is one with that name, but that was not the point. The point was that I could see it coming. It was like the cycle of seasons: old man winter, youthful spring, lusty summer, chilly autumn. And leaves fell, snow covered the sidewalk, and flowers bloomed as we sat there with menus in our hands, wait people hesitating, waiting for the heartbreak to end, so they could tell us the special of the day was Shmuck Elke, yours truly sautéed and skewered, served on a bed of rice pilaf.

There was always the sound of silverware clinking on china as my heart broke. It didn't do this noisily. Not like a busboy dropping a tray of dirty dishes—the clatter, the shatter of it. Not like that. More like what follows: The sudden hush. I heard it then. The shatter was Elke's foreign voice. Who was she? I had no idea. A year later I would not be able to spot her in a crowd. And even if I did, she'd pretend not to see me, even were I to be standing there on my tiptoes, waving with both hands like a fool.

"Really," said Elke. "I can see the future." Elke continued braiding her hair, glancing lazily about the dining room, trying to focus on someone more interesting than me, another bright fellow who would humiliate himself for her. "We would never work out. I think we'd be like a piece of gum."

Juicy fruit? Double bubble? Trident? *The brand that four out of five dentists recommend for their patients who chew gum?*

She claimed the flavor was not important. It's more a matter of texture. Of feeling. "You know. At first chewing gum is all sweet juiciness. You love to have it in your mouth. Sliding against your tongue." She closed her eyes and made a swooning face, the tongue-across-the-lips, Pearl Drops routine. "But that doesn't last long. Then you reach some point when it starts to turn bad. It starts to feel like a disgusting thing in your mouth. And you can't spit it out. It just won't stop. It's just there, you know? Relentless. At some point you hate it." The next look she gave me was pure Gross Out. "At some point it begins to feel like you're chewing a midget's kidney."

She lifted her napkin to her lips and dabbed. Her eyes focused on a table of six Wall Street types, all belly laughs and take-no-prisoners. I considered plunging my fork into her throat. Just a thought.

— — —

As the account review loomed closer, I did my best to block out June and Elke, keeping only Mia close to my skin and bones, locking myself in the grip of This Whatever We Have, my heart filled with nothing but her and my mind concentrated on coffee. She spent most of her nights at my place, giving it life: Mia in bed, with the white cotton sheet wrapped around her head, like an old woman's shawl, a mischievous look on her face, smiling at me, saying, "Have you seen the baby Jesus?" When she cooked dinner for me, she always began by sautéing onions and garlic, standing over the cutting board, her hair pulled back, done in that I'm-a-nice-girl French braid, casting curly shadows on the wall beside her. When she was not around, there were always mementoes to remember her by: her peppermint foot lotion in the shower stall, her white bra in my magazine basket.

We couldn't find a name to fit our relationship. It was secret, and for a time, we liked the label forbidden. The ring of *taboo*. But as we came to care more for each other, things got tangled and messy, and none of the terms hit the mark. *Affair* implied the whole husbands-and-wives thing, *fling* sounded like something litterbugs do. The L word, for a variety of reasons, seemed off limits. A padlock on the gate, a sign warning THIS PROPERTY PROTECTED BY GUARD DOGS. Once, in a conversation, cozy and warm with her in bed, I said, "I don't know what to think of it, this whatever we have, but I like it." The name stuck.

She helped with the testimonials.

"I want a cup of coffee that will knock my socks off and put the fear of god in me again."

"I want a cup of coffee that will do my taxes and return the phone calls of all those people I've been meaning to get back to but never have time to fit in my busy schedule they're far away and you know what they say out of sight out of mind."

She made me dizzy: the joy of sleeping beside the warm limbs—arms, legs, breasts, belly—of a lovely naked woman. Her warm skin. The alluring, shrimpy steam of her pudenda. As she fell asleep, I would scratch her back. As she dreamed of ex-girlfriends, I would slip my fingers down the cheeks of her bottom, grazing the tender, shaven skin of her sex.

When she came to bed, she loosened her hair and it sprayed out over her shoulders, long and wavy, her body lithe and willowy, her shoulders narrow and her hips wide. Her breasts were small but gently round, and she stood naked, putting a CD in the player, asking what I wanted to hear, thrusting out her belly. She did not hurry. I admired her nakedness. She liked this. Liked me looking at her skin. When she returned to bed she slid into my arms, smiling at me, saying, "You are the sweet one, aren't you?" I kissed her eyelids and eyelashes. She came with me inside her, her fingers on her clit, her limbs lurching as if she were guinea-pigging for electroshock treatments: ask and ye shall receive.

As we fell to sleep she whispered, "I want a cup of coffee that will fuck me silly and do the dishes while I read the movie reviews."

– – –

The day before we were to pitch our campaigns to Cameron, office scuttlebutt via Shelly Curapada had it that June was in Cameron's office for two hours, saying I was having an affair with Elke and possibly "other employees." If I wasn't fired, June threatened to file a class-action lawsuit on behalf of the women in the office, victims of my unwarranted sexual advances. Even those who asserted it was consensual were coerced into the sexual relationship with me for fear of losing their jobs, or did so in an attempt to curry favor and gain promotions.

In the aftermath of this meeting, amid the rumor and hubbub, Mia fucked me like you wouldn't believe. Like she had something to prove. Like let's give them something to talk about. It started when she straddled me on the couch, and when we decided to move upstairs to the bedroom, she locked her legs around me tight, and I stood up, still inside of her. I had to blow out the candles as we left the room, and squatting down to blow out the flame, felt myself slipping out, saying, "Oh, dang."

"Close," she said. "You get an A for effort."

Blowing out the candle, I splashed candle wax on my feet and legs, gasping in pain. She spilled her drink across my back and laughed till she broke into a coughing fit. When I came, my vision polka-dotted with purple spots, as if I could see the very corpuscles of my plasma exploding like cartoon bombs. In that moment, I didn't care about the Risk. I didn't care about the Others. I only cared about This Whatever We Have.

As long as I could see her the next night, I didn't care what they did to me. Throw me in the slammer. Drag me to the dungeon. Lock me in my cell. I'll spit at the guards and throw my metal plate of gruel against the stone wall. Fuck you all, fuck all of you. I don't care. You heard me right. I don't care. I am beyond the edge. In that moment, as she clawed me to sleep, I had Wile E. Coyote written all over me: I just didn't care. With a foolish grin on my face and the expectation of further frames to be drawn, I saw the canyon floor rushing toward me.

— — —

Mia and I were the last creative team to go. The others were all slick and polished, but ours had nerve. When it was time to stand

and deliver, I showed Mia a note I had just scrawled. "Fuck art. Let's dance!" As we pitched it, Cameron watched with seeming indifference. When we finished speaking, the room was silent. Elke smoothed her hair away from her cheeks and wondered just who was most in love with her. June did her typical rendition of a barely controlled antidepressant slow burn. Richard crossed his fingers for us. And finally Cameron said, "I want a cup of coffee that will splash my face with cold water and tell me I'm beautiful?" He grinned. "Now that's good." He looked around the room for other reactions. "June? What do you think?"

She removed her glasses and polished them with a Kleenex. Her keep-them-waiting shtick. "I don't get the point."

Cameron gave her a penetrating look, his chin held high, then nodded. "Enough. We'll talk later." He then stood and came to shake hands with both of us, telling everyone that this is what he'd lead off with, directing a pecking order to the others he'd fall back on if the client didn't like it. As the meeting broke up, he headed off for lunch with Elke, and asked Richard to see that the necessary arrangements were made for tomorrow's conference, adding that since June seemed disinterested in the chosen campaign, see that she didn't attend the pitch. I heard him say, "Her negative energy might pollute the psychic waters."

Back in my office, with the door closed, Mia literally hopped upon me, wrapping her arms around my neck and her legs around my hips. She said, "You know what? My toes are itching something fierce."

—  —  —

To celebrate the success of our account review, Cameron chartered a Circle Line cruise around Manhattan, which some of us followed with a night on the town: *Come on along and take me to/The lullaby of Broadway.* It was all-aboard on a blustery afternoon. Seagulls hovered and dipped in the fishy-smelling air above us. The gusty wind blew my hair in my face, flags popped along the docks, and Richard leaned close to shout, "Word on the street is, June is history!"

I smiled and said, "And April is supposed to be cruel, isn't it?" I also reminded him that May usually saw an upturn in the hotly contested retail clothing market. He had just been given responsibility for the Tommy Hilfiger account, and needed to think Fashion.

Mia was there, camera in one hand and cigarette in the other, her hair pinned up and tumbling down in seventies retro prom-night curls, lipstick bright as candy apples, eyelashes as long as ever. We sipped champagne in coffee mugs and struggled to refrain from conspicuous gloating. People slapped me on the back and gave me looks that began in Surprise, passed through Admiration, and arrived at Envy.

Elke made a heart-stopping entrance, walking slow-mo down the gangplank, giving me the whammy. She looked to-die-for in a black-and-white, Pierre Mondrian dress, sporting a new do—blonde locks cut in swirls and arcing bangs hanging in her eyes—Veronica Lake Does Dondi, copycatting Elaine from a *Seinfeld* episode.

"Who are you?" she asked. "The cat's meow?"

I shrugged. "I'm more like a rock," I said. "You might even think of me as an island."

She smirked. "And will your poetry protect you?"

Mia squeezed between us, taking pictures of everyone with her digital, playing Annie Leibovitz. "Say *That's not my husband, that's my stalker!*" She left my eyes scored with paparazzi spots, but it was a welcome interruption. As we pulled away from the West Side docks, below us the props swirled a frothy wake in the gray waters of the Hudson, their churn threatening to bring the bodies of mob informants to the surface. We looked away. We didn't need to see that. Nobody likes a snitch. Soon the lovely menace was posing promo stills for *All About Elke!* Mia saved my skin. It was all I could do not to squeeze her. We could keep a secret. We could keep This Whatever We Have to ourselves. I grinned like the luckiest of all. As we passed the Statue of Liberty, the sky above swarmed with gulls, and like a java junkie after a fix, the world seemed jittery with hope.

# The Next Worst Thing

The worst thing about fights and I when I say *fights* I don't mean disagreements I mean someone slamming a crowbar against your windshield because you've got the doors locked you keep trying to start the car dropping the keys scrabbling for them on the floorboards this heavy feeling in your bones it's hard to move your hands arms tongue fingers gone spasmo meanwhile this happening in a heartbeat the diplomat outside is still swinging that crowbar *Who do you think you're fucking with?* he screams you wince at the bashing sound as the windshield spiderwebs & starts to sag he keeps shouting *I told you to get out of the fucking car! I told you! Get out of the fucking car!*

I don't mean disagreements like maybe you like salted pretzels and someone else doesn't not that at all you know what I'm saying. What I'm saying is . . . the worst thing about fights is that moment when it begins or it's about to begin and there's someone standing in your face right in front of you he wants to hurt you badly fuck you up mangle your face break your nose or put one of your eyes out maybe cause you serious pain reduce you to drooling bloody on your hands and knees in gravel.

Have you ever had a fist or a boot slam into your belly? It crushes you to the ground where they'll kick your teeth out I swear it happens people will kick you in the *mouth*. In Billings, Montana, I once saw a bar fight where some boozy, purple-nosed cowboy grabbed this wasted longhair by his ponytail yanked dragged his entire body by the hair outside, pulling him backward into the parking lot, put the guy's face against a concrete curb and kicked the back of it. I was in the crowd watching. We shouted for him to cut it out but we didn't step in to stop it. We weren't stupid. We didn't want a taste of the same medicine. We had our own teeth to keep an eye on. Keep your mouth shut and you won't get hurt. But still it made me sick to see it hear it. The sound when boot smacked head. I mean it could have been me, you know what I'm saying? It was a wet, muffled crunch, like a stepping on a raw egg in your socks.

— — —

But the last fight I was in was my fault sort of at least partially he'd been screwing my wife and humiliated me at a party I didn't find out about the wife-screwing part of it until later but everyone at the party probably knew it sure they knew it and all thought me = chump.

But it's not like I was a saint or anything we were separated at the time me and my wife that is and I suspected she was seeing someone so was I and oh well you know I asked for it I moved out on her but this genius made a point of rubbing my nose in it I would never have known but he wanted me to know I mean I'm sure he was saying to people I work with people I have lunch with eat pizza with, "Guess whose wife I'm poking?"

He said that I knew he did it got back to me but that wasn't the worst part the worst part was when I learned about it the next day after the party that he'd been mouthing off about me I ask my wife,

"So what was all that between you and Sigmund last night?"

I know I know Sigmund as in Freud a lot of people didn't like him he was the kind of guy who seemed okay at first good-looking but short quiet and moody brooding I think they call it you might have liked him the first few times you saw him until you got to know him and learned what an asshole he was so I ask what was his problem at the party and my wife Dianne's her name says, "Never mind. He's just hot air. Don't pay any attention to him."

But I could tell something was up by the way she said it and we were getting back together I mean the next week I was moving back in with her I loved this woman like you love your hands your eyeballs your teeth for that matter something you can't live without. We keep hashing it over & when I finally put two and two together I ask, "What? Did you sleep with him?"

"Don't ask me any questions unless you want to hear the truth. I'm not going to lie."

"Okay so I'm asking you."

"Gary. Don't start anything."

"I'm asking if you slept with him. If you did I should know right?"

"We've been separated for a year, Gary. You asked for it."

And I was thinking *Jesus*, not *him*, anyone but *him*, Sigmund that little squirmy shit but what I said was, "Did you or didn't you? Let's get this straight."

"I don't like your tone of voice. Who moved out on who, tell me that?"

"Either you did or you didn't. Yes or no."

It took a while but I pulled it out of her ripped it from her like that monster in *Alien* you know that slimy worm thing with huge teeth that erupts out of the guy's chest at breakfast and splatters goo and disgusting shit all over everybody so I pulled it out of her and that was bad enough suddenly it was like playing on video monitors in my mind. But the worst thing was then she told me she didn't really want to do it he was so *pushy* she said he kind of forced her he lifted weights he was short but worked out classic Napoleon complex he was so strong she said and I know Dianne believe me she wasn't lying I never doubted her one minute she's a straight shooter the real thing she's got her flaws sure don't we all but she doesn't lie she doesn't make things up I mean she's just not the lying type so I ask, "Did he rape you?"

"No, not really. I gave in, I guess. But he was so *pushy*. He just wouldn't take no for an answer."

"How many times?"

"Gary. No."

"It's important. Was this months or what?"

"Just twice or three times I think. Three I guess. Something like that. I hadn't heard from him for months, but lately he's been calling and has become so pushy again. I told him I can't see him anymore that we're getting back together and everything but he says you're no good for me that we shouldn't move back in together and I'm afraid of him, Gary. I really am. He's violent. He's a violent person and he drinks a lot. I don't think he'd really hurt me but I don't know, he's a scary guy. I shouldn't have done it, I know, but you left me and he's the only one who asked me out so what was I supposed to do stay home all the time he seemed so nice at first."

And that was it. When she told me she was scared of him that the woman I love and not only that but who happens to be without a doubt one of the best people I know in the world kind & sweet & gentle so when I learned this beautiful gentle & tender human being was scared of this little fuck I went nuts it threw me over the edge and it was like, "Where does he live?"

"Gary it's over and done with and—"

"Where does he live?"

"I'm not going to tell you that. I don't want to see you get hurt he's got guns knives he's that kind of guy it's over I'm telling you I love you."

"It is not over. What about last night? What was that all about?"

"He was just trying to mess with you he hates you Gary. You wouldn't believe the things he says about you. He said if you loved me you wouldn't let him go near me. He was talking to me all last night and you didn't do a thing about it."

"He told you this last night?"

"If you'd just told him to leave me alone he probably would have."

"He wanted me to start something with him at a party full of people friends of mine?"

"He's just a pest."

"Why didn't you just walk away from him?"

"I did, but you were talking to that Betty woman. What was I supposed to do, huh? He followed me everywhere. He was so drunk he made me miserable and you were no help."

"You could have—"

"I'm afraid of him Gary and I don't want him to hurt you."

"I'm gonna give that little shit something to be afraid of. I'm going to teach that little shit to squirm."

"He could hurt you."

"I don't care!"

I slammed my fist in the bedroom door hooked my hand into it and jerked back ripping my skin trying to slam it only I'd yanked it bent from the hinges on the wall so it wouldn't slam I go to the phone & start calling people trying to sound calm trying to keep my shit together. I had to leave my stupid voice on answering machines, dial another number, pace back and forth in Dianne's living room, waiting for people to return the calls. It was afternoon by this time, a Sunday, and since Dianne lived near a softball field, there were kids walking by in groups of twos and threes carrying bats and gloves, tossing balls into the air and catching them as they passed her house.

It was a gorgeous day—blue sky, green leaves, the country at peace. They laughed and jostled each other, carried the bats over their shoulders like clubs. Inside my head were bloodstains splattered on wallpaper. It was hard to reach people on the phone, and once I got them, hard to get any information from them. They didn't want to deal with me. They didn't want to get involved. They'd say stuff like, "Listen, man, this has nothing to do with me, okay? So I can't tell you anything." I'd usually start yelling at them about that point, which worked so well they hung up. But finally someone gave me his number. "You don't tell him where you got this, okay?"

— — —

When I get Sigmund on the phone he says,

"Listen man, sorry about last night. I was out of line, I know that. I was drunk, man. I just had too much and I didn't know what—"

"You were out of line. Is that it?"

"You don't have to shout, okay? I mean, I know I made an ass of myself."

"You fucked my wife you motherfucker and you say you were out of line?"

He hung up I called right back and he said, "Don't yell at me."

"I'll do whatever the fuck I want asshole."

"Would you stop screaming? Listen, I'm sorry."

"Sorry's not good enough. You humiliate me, you hassle my wife at a party full of my friends, then say you're sorry? Fuck sorry! You want to fight, is that it? Okay motherfucker, you got your wish. Let's meet somewhere right now and get this over with."

"I don't want to fight you."

"You scare my wife and talk shit about me you don't have a choice, asshole."

"Listen."

"What are you, chicken?"

"Don't call me—"

"You're a coward is what you are a miserable little drunken fuck coward."

"I'm not going to fight you—"

"Now or later asshole let's get this thing over with I'm getting ready to move back with my wife and you make sure I find out how you fucked her well you better—"

—    —    —

After that he hangs up I quit screaming realizing that my psycho drug dealer neighbors must surely be overhearing it all slam the phone against the coffee table grab the cord and swing the mouthpiece in the air smash it against the floor then pull it apart with my hands until it's ripped to pieces. After I rip the cord from the wall and fling the pieces of plastic and wiring across the room I pace back and forth, aware that now I can't call him back from home. I have to use the pay phone at the 7-Eleven down the block, like every other deadbeat in the 'hood.

I stomp over there passing poor ladies at the bus stop who look scared of me and I stand in the parking lot full of oil stains & broken glass call him on the skuzzy pay phone and hiss into it. He hangs up again so I call his friends and threaten them too. I keep calling I don't give up and finally get him pissed off and he says, "Okay motherfucker you asked for it."

—    —    —

Like I said I was no saint I mean I never thought I was *evil* or anything I've always considered myself an honest person well for the most part basically a good person I think but I've done some crummy things. Right about that same time I was seeing a married woman myself *having an affair* they call it sounds like a dinner gala fund raiser for homeless opera singers caviar & champagne *Don't spill the Swedish meatballs on your tux, Nigel!*

But no our affair wasn't like that more like raw hot serious dizzy intense blush-about-it-later screwing whenever & wherever we got a chance in public mostly but the woman let's call her Beth I did like When can I see you again Beth? as we sat in weird bars on the outskirts of Phoenix drinking margaritas salt on her lips wrought iron bullshit on the walls getting looped & horny we would fuck like anywhere semi-alone & dark the Planetarium was a good one all the stars above and my pants unzipped.

Most of the time we did it in her car a Camry, Car of the Year. We'd hunker down in deserted parking lots, those huge saguaro cactus outside looking like big green men watching us. If you drove by all you'd see was a car, a late-model Toyota, parked in an empty lot, in the desert. You wouldn't see that I had my pants yanked down to my ankles.

By the time this happened with Sigmund, I was feeling pretty bad about it, had decided to end it, move back with Dianne. I mean Beth was quote unquote fun odd word to describe adultery, yes? But her being married made the whole thing major sordid. I mean, we'd tell each other next time we're just having lunch, okay? No touching, no fooling around. We like each other, we can be just friends, can't we? But then we'd meet at Gordo's or Los Huerfanos and by the second margarita or halfway through the third I'd be watching her lips on the glass I'd be staring at her face so lovely young twenty-three she was a school teacher fifth grade & fresh and even the way her teeth were funky these weird dingy streaks on them & overlapping a bit even that was sexy because she was real who wants perfection anyway & her eyes were green with gold flecks in them like topaz yeah that's it.

Topaz eyes she had hair in ringlets blond and fine like sewing thread she got it permed regularly and for all the world looked like one of the local anchorwomen on Eyewitness News so that when we'd be doing it sometimes I imagined the anchor lady like smorgasbord on the table of her news desk I never thought all that perming was good for her but what was I to do I couldn't very well tell her how to dress or wear her hair now could I?

Blonde permed hair and pantyhose stiff as chain mail that's what I remember about Beth. But she was a beautiful person, too. I mean when you say *adultery* people tend to think of vicious oversexed bored hausfraus cuckolding their workaday hubbies but she wasn't like that at all. She was sweet & good & we never meant it to happen. It just did. We'd known & lusted after each other a year before we fell. We all make mistakes don't we? We always felt guilty afterward we'd swear *never again* but we'd miss each other within hours call on the phone and say, "We'll just have lunch, okay? Nothing more than that."

"Just lunch."

After the drinks I'd touch her wrist or her pantyhose or hold her hand beneath the tablecloth & we'd fall again we'd see each other falling but like a telephone we'd take our consciences off the hook ignore the buzzer and after paying cash for the drinks no Visa or Mastercard like normal no cash so they couldn't trace us I'd go to the men's room before we left the cafe and stuff a handful of paper towels or maybe a sheaf of paper napkins grabbed from an empty table in my pocket to clean up after I came later in the car. But sometimes still it got on the upholstery. Beth's Car of the Year had sex stains on the seat. Did her husband ever notice them? He liked to take the bus he did he was civic minded he took the bus to work every day meanwhile Beth and I are sweating and pink in their car. Not something to be proud of. I thought about that. What if my wife did that? Then I didn't think about it anymore too creepy to imagine, a guilt surge shorting out my conscience.

— — —

It bothered Beth, too. Beth I called her, as in, "Beth, you make me feel so alive." But really everyone else in her life called her *Betty*. She was Betty at school in the teacher's lounge Betty to her husband Dick I kid you not. She was Betty to her father dying of pancreatic cancer. She was Betty teaching ten year olds in Tempe, with a yellow bow in her hair, wearing an impossibly long dress looking like a schoolmarm from *Little House on the Prairie*. But when I was with her, when we were alone, she was Beth. She was Beth when she undid my pants in the parking lot of La Casa Escondida and stroked me. She was Beth when she kissed it. She was Betty full of guilt when she scrubbed her Car of the Year, trying to erase the stains.

At the time to make matters worse she was newly married lived in this suburban house in the desert. Green cactus garden and white concrete drive in her front yard. The place was so new you could still smell the shower curtains. And no furniture. I mean I'm not Martha Stewart or anything but this house was *bare*. The living room was *completely* empty, not a stick the walls bare & white the carpeting green as frozen margaritas. There were curtains yes there were curtains, but as we squirmed naked on the bare green carpeting of the living room I stared at walls of nothing. No posters, no photos, no seascapes. Nothing. Only, near the baseboard, two electrical outlets, like eyes.

I'd sneak over in the afternoons. We'd meet there with the blinds drawn. Her neighbors were space aliens for all we knew. And we'd do it in the empty living room on that green shag carpeting. She'd lay out a blanket to keep me from getting knee burns. That way, doing it on the living room floor, we didn't mess up her marriage bed, where she slept with Dick every night. Nothing would stop us, though, nothing. I hope god forgives me for that. I really do.

— — —

Beth didn't like the idea of me moving back with Dianne.

"How do you think that makes me feel?" she asked me. "You're breaking my heart."

She wanted us to divorce both and get together but I wasn't sure. Sometimes I thought she was too silly and dim and that after all that trouble we'd get together and I'd just end up cheating on her. I know something about myself. I know I can never get enough. I never said I loved her I never said it. That means something, doesn't it? So we were calling it quits at least supposedly when I moved back in a deadline of sorts though I saw her the day before that party parking lot fellatio oh well the flesh is weak but later after everything I never told her about what happened I didn't know how it would make her feel I didn't know.

— — —

Talking on the pay phone at 7-Eleven standing in a shatter of broken beer bottles I listen as Sigmund agrees to meet me at a city park telling me, "Don't bring a gun."

I spit back that I don't *own* one I knew he did though he'd told me about the shotgun he'd bought only two days before I didn't care I didn't *care*.

— — —

I arrived early at the park and scoped out a clump of oak trees that were away from the parked cars, the crowds of children, the picnic tables. I was waiting by a statue of a cowboy hero some wrangler armed with Bowie knife and Winchester when he pulled into the parking got out of the car stiff as the weight lifter he was and walked toward me wearing jeans a tight white t-shirt a cap. He was a lot stockier, beefier, stronger than me.

I told him to follow me to the trees & he did lagging several yards behind till we reached the trees & I turned around and told him, "Go ahead. C'mon, let's do it."

He'd said I was a coward for not being willing to fight him. He'd told this to a woman I loved. He'd said this at a party peopled with my friends and co-workers everyone had known what he'd done his pointing out what a weakling I was what a wimp I was so here I am go ahead you sonofabitch you want to fight let's do it you humiliate me in front of a room full of people well it's just the two of us now *fucker* let's go for it.

He told me he was sorry.

Sorry!

He didn't mean it he was sorry he told me he didn't want to fight.

"Really, man. I was drunk. I didn't mean it. I don't even remember what I said."

The sun was hot the air was dry and I screamed at him I didn't *care* and raised my fists coming close to him and he raised his arms & flinched to keep away from me that's when I started swinging he ducked and turned away from me I didn't seem to connect to anything but air then I hit him several times quickly. He made a squeaky, pained sound with each blow. He ducked to the ground where I beat my fists against his back, then I kicked him as hard as I could in his ribs. He squirmed on the ground, coughing. He wasn't fighting back. He would not get up and would not defend himself even when I told him to. His cap was knocked off his head into the sandy dirt. I remember thinking that I wanted to grab it and rip it in two. He hugged his ribs in pain on his knees before me and for a moment I thought to kick him in the teeth. I was wearing heavy leather boots I almost did it. Almost.

— — —

I circled him, screaming, as he struggled to his feet, picked up his cap, & limped away toward the parking lot.

I walked around in a circle, cussing and panting, out of breath from anger and raw a*dreeno*. For the first time I noticed all the litter around us, red and white Coke cups and corn dog sticks, buzzing flies. Three men at a picnic table about thirty yards away were watching me. I started to sob, still punching the air. After circling the trees near our clearing for several minutes, I walked away and headed deeper into the park.

— — —

It was spring, and had rained recently, so as I walked through the thicket of oaks and pines I stared down at the clay mud, the crisscross hatching of fallen reddish brown pine needles, the puddles burnt orange with muddy clay water. In the shadows, a dark red. The air was full of dragonflies. I walked blindly, not caring where I was going, feeling as if something inside me had changed, realizing something serious had happened. Perhaps I walked into the park to get away from myself. I felt dirty and ugly. I wondered if the police would be coming after me. I walked and walked. My boots became caked with red mud. I somehow managed to reach a nature trail, which had numbered plaques identifying the different trees in the park: the white pine, the live oak, the hackberry. Yucca, saguaro, century plant. All around zinged dragonflies.

After a while I emerged from the pine forest nature trail and onto a jogging path. A few of the passing joggers gave me looks. Maybe because I was a walker on the running trail, maybe because I looked like a lunatic. I had the feeling that everyone *knew*. I certainly didn't look like I belonged there. I wore an old flannel shirt and blue jeans, the heavy boots caked with mud. I felt like an ax murderer, as if I were covered with splatters of blood like I'd just dumped a body raped bruised strangled beaten in a shallow grave two tree-huggers would find later & they'd have to identify by dental records young Caucasian female last seen in a convenience store eleven o'clock at night talking to a man in a red pickup. It always goes something like that.

— — —

He took it like a man.

As I wound my slow and clumsy way down the three-mile jogging path, passed by runners in Nikes, singlets, and fluorescent pink running shorts, I was haunted by what I'd just done, how I had just pounded on a person who had not even tried to defend himself. That was the kicker. I couldn't say I had won anything. Some fight. Knowing he probably could have hurt me fucked me up seriously made it even worse, like I was so insignificant he would let me pound him and walk away no big deal. No scarier than the dragonflies buzzing in the air around my face.

— — —

The jogging path brought me back full circle to the center of the park, and to reach my car, I had to cross the saddest zoo in the world. A squad of prickly pear bloomed brightly, red and yellow, in a row as I rounded a turn, crossed a wooden bridge over a muddy duck stream to enter the zoo. It was small and low budget. The kind of zoo that can only afford one of everything, where baboons masturbate behind bars like juvenile delinquents on display. A great target for grade school field trips. After I passed through the teeth of the metal turnstiles, I had to pause as a dwarf train chugged by on its narrow tracks. It was crammed with kids, and the few parents aboard looked like clumsy giants—the whole thing done to resemble a circus caravan—crude lions, giraffes, and elephants painted on the sides of each tiny car. The children waved to me, and I waved back. The kid's laughter rang through the air of the small zoo, and the train's conductor gave its weak whistle a blast as it neared the pedestrian pathway.

I bought a Coke in a red and white paper cup, drank it as I stood beside the sea lion pool, trying to wedge my way between the eight year olds to catch a glimpse of the lions tossing beach balls into the air with their noses, their whiskered faces. A security guard strolled by.

— — —

Through all this—the zoo, the sea lions, the next few weeks—my mind involuntarily instant-replayed visions of the fight. Swinging wildly at him. Pummeling his back. The high-pitched, squeaking sound he made when I hit him. His cap in the mud. My reaction went through stages. A few days later, I learned Sigmund had a black eye and cracked sternum. *Good*, I thought, *but that isn't enough*. I worried that he'd sue me. I felt guilty again. Because of his sternum, he had trouble breathing. It hurt each time he drew a breath. It would take several months to heal. Good. *Good*.

And inside me swelled disgust.

— — —

After the fight I went home and sat in the living room of my rented apartment. Low ceilings squeezed me like a vise. Pigeons cooed and humped in the eaves of the windows. Dust clouds drifted across the hardwood floors. The mentholatum smell of my landlord rose from his apartment below. Pieces of the phone were still scattered across the floor: wires, mouthpiece, a circular metal plate with holes drilled in it. If Sigmund wanted to get back at me, to get revenge, this was not a good place to wait. Alone there I was a sitting duck. I threw some things in a duffel, stopped at the 7-Eleven to use the phone again, called a friend in Flagstaff and drove there. It became cooler as I drove into the mountains, the woods thick with trees, and I slowed to keep from hitting a mule deer. At my friend's place, I stayed a week, watching TV and trying to joke about it. Over the phone I'd told him the basics. When I arrived he said, "Well if it isn't Muhammad Ali."

– – –

He made me feel better, my friend did, human again, and after a few days it seemed okay. I called Dianne and we had a long talk. I would move back in anyway. We wouldn't let this stupid crap ruin everything. But when I returned to Phoenix I learned that while I was out of town Sigmund kept calling her at five and six o'clock in the morning, after he'd been drinking all night and she was getting up to go to work. He'd be calling, wanting to talk.

"All I want to do is talk. How you doing? I miss you."

She told me he said that and she was scared. He told her he was fixing some pay-back and I better buy some eyes to put in the back of my head if I wanted to see it coming. So with him still messing with me & her when I got back in town and moved back home with her I came up with a plan. I knew what I'd do if he messed with me any more. I couldn't just take it, could I?

– – –

I bought a gun from an ex-con I knew, a .45 caliber military looking thing. It set me back five hundred dollars but I figured it was worth it. Peace of mind.

"Nobody fuck with you if you point this thing at 'em," said the guy I bought it from. "They know who the boss is."

– – –

At first I really didn't like the idea but it felt surprisingly good in my hand it felt hard a real confidence builder it was and we all need that don't we confidence I mean I wouldn't want anyone thinking I'm some loser they can just push around but I got this piece clean, no papers no serial number no nothing. I thought about this a lot.

I decided that, if he kept it up, one night I'd go over to his apartment complex some maximum-security type thing off Van Buren. You know, near the singles bar strip. I'd wait till someone opens the outer gates and follow after them my face hidden hooded sweatshirt sweatpants on like I'm a jogger just coming back forgot my keys thanks a lot. I know he's home so I wait in the parking lot till he goes out to his car to leave I scoped out the lot beforehand and there was a perfect place behind the dumpster in the shadows of it smelled bad though gag me but it had a perfect angle to scope out Sigmund's car always parked in the same assigned place.

I wear a ski mask under the sweatshirt hood gloves even wrap my shoes in duct tape so they can't trace any prints & then he comes out.

I let him open the car door before I move, .45 in my right hand, loose but firm, homemade silencer over the barrel three condoms how appropriate, it takes seven steps to reach him his car door and he's already in has his right hand on the key in the ignition his left hand cranking the window down as I sneak up silent-like and point the gun at his ear squeeze the trigger.

His head jerks to the side hard to see for a moment his body in shadows but he lifts his head back up he's not dead & then I see the bullet hit below his ear and bones and blood are there open on the side of his face this jagged thing sticking out which I realize is his jawbone smashed but he's still alive he's trying to breathe turns his face toward me blood coming out his nose it blows a fat red bubble then pops I point & shoot him again this time in the eye his head popping back and this time he doesn't lift back up but I go ahead and put three more bullets into his chest to make sure he'll never squawk about my wife again who the fuck does he think he is anyway?

— — —

I decided that's what I'd do, if he kept pressing me. And it came to pass that Sigmund ended up dead. Found in the front seat of his car, bullet holes and all. The cops came to the house and asked me questions. They took notes about my answers. And left.

They never returned. About two million people hated Sigmund. He owed money to drug dealers and the police probably figured Why bother?

That wasn't the end of everything. I still lost Dianne over my stupidity. And goddamnit, I loved her so much! I really did. The best thing that ever happened to me. She was. She found out about it, of course, they always do. *It* as in Beth and what we did in her Car of the Year. But about Sigmund she wondered of course. One of the last times I saw her we had lunch at our favorite diner. I remember almost crying when the waitress put the a tuna melt dead on a white plate in front of me, like I could hear some countdown to missing Dianne already, when out of the blue she asks, "So. Was it you?"

"Was it me what?"

"You know."

"What? You think I'm that stupid?"

"If it was you I should know, right? I have a right. So just tell me. Yes or no."

I asked how was her chicken salad. She just stares at me finally she goes, "Okay. Okay. If you had anything to do with that I don't want to know I don't *even* want to know."

I didn't end it with Beth till she quit answering my calls. Once she asked me, "Can't you get the picture?" I think she's back to being Betty. I think she's Betty full time now. And I hope she's happy. I really do.

But truth be told, it's not that hard to kill a guy. Really it's not. You can get away with murder. You drive home, lock your door and put your keys and coins on the dresser, home again home again jiggedy jig. You cope. After a while, you move on to some new fuck-up in your life. The next worst thing. You forget, until something reminds you. The laughter of children. Image of kids on a tiny train. The smell of elephant dung at a crummy zoo. The cry of a peacock. You try to forget, to tell yourself that it didn't happen to you, that it's in the past now. Spilled milk. Until one day you see someone glaring at you with vengeance in his eyes.

# What Happens to Rain?

What happened then was not a noble thing or a brave thing or an event that might some day be described on a plaque forged by the fat hands of a Chamber of Commerce. What happened then was more like a mistake wrapped in a bloody bundle of paper towels and rushed to the hospital in a hurry with faint hope that it could all be made right again good as new. What happened took place in a town full of cowboys and ranchers and rich people who liked to ski. It was a town of wide streets, utility sheds, log cabin shacks, and dream homes. It was at the edge of the Great Plains. In the west there were mountains.

The stuffed heads of elk and mule deer hung in the supermarkets. The convenience stores sold gasoline, milk, and chewing tobacco. There were churches, banks, and schools. In the back of a tenth-grade class in the high school, a dusty class with dirty white floor tiles, dirty white ceiling tiles, and graffiti-scarred brown school desks, sat Mouse Foley. She had a good heart, but she was not the brightest light. Her real name was Hannah.

She had her finger in her right ear, wiggling it. She liked the squishy sound it made. Rick Penny told everyone to check it out; Mouse is doing it to her ear. When the other students turned to look, Mouse removed her finger and hung down her head, her asphalt-black hair shrouding her face. She moved her hands to look busy and knocked a pencil off her desk. It rolled away like a friend embarrassed to be seen with her. Without comment, Bonnie Esposito leaned over, picked it up, and placed it back on the desk.

At the age of fifteen, Mouse could barely spell and add. She had a lazy eye, which gave her face the effect that she was cross-eyed. Plus she was a big girl, over six feet tall, with big feet, a strong chin, sharp nose and prominent cheekbones, dark, thick eyebrows. She should have been in Special Education classes. The teachers defined her as "slow." But the school district had done away with Special Education and had instituted the idea of mainstreaming. Now the slow children were mixed in with the normal or quick children, which was supposed to be better for them, the slow ones. That way they could fit in. But everyone always knew who was slow, who was easy to pick on. When Mouse tried to read, she leaned over the desk and stared at the words very carefully and closely. Her tongue protruded from the side of her mouth. She had an IQ of 78.

When her mother, Dora, read the letter that informed her of that, she frowned and said, "That doesn't mean anything. You're just different. That's all." She washed the dishes and stared out the window. "I know a lot of smart people who are ugly and mean. The world would be better off without them. You're a sweetheart. Not that it makes it any easier. Worse, maybe. But it's something."

"Sweetheart," said Mouse.

—  —  —

At William Tecumseh Sherman High School the only person who offered Mouse kindness and consideration was Mr. Lawrence, the janitor and groundskeeper. Nestled inside Mr. Lawrence's left ear was a brown plastic hearing aid, an outdated kind, like a robotic crab curled into the conch shell of his ear. The old device no longer worked well. If he happened to be mopping the halls when class changed he seemed oblivious to the throng of passing teenagers. His mop water filled the air with a strong ammonia smell. Students walked by, jeering and laughing. They shouted, "Hey, Quasimodo! What are you trying to do? Give us a nose bleed?" They said they were going to slip and break their necks, then sue the school and make Mr. Lawrence lose his job. "Then they'll put you back in the dungeon with the other freaks," they said.

Mr. Lawrence showed Mouse his private room behind the gymnasium, in the utility shed that housed the lawnmowers and snowblowers. It was their secret. He fed Mouse peanut butter cookies and bottles of warm root beer that foamed and bubbled out furiously, that left a funny mustache on her face, which she licked off her lips with her tongue. He bought her a white nurse's uniform as a present and told her she could pretend to take his blood pressure and give him a tuberculosis vaccine. She asked what was tuberculosis? What was blood pressure?

Mr. Lawrence told her to never mind. He had her put on the nurse's uniform and model it for him. It was so crisp and white! And there was a hat! Mouse loved hats. She walked back and forth, transforming the cement floor in the small, corrugated metal building into the catwalk of a fashion show. Mr. Lawrence sat on the wooden stool in front of the buzzing, glowing-orange grid of the electric space heater and watched fondly. He shook his head and told her she was so beautiful. He didn't know what to do about it. People were so unfair. Life was so unfair. He said she was so beautiful he could kiss her.

"Please," said Mouse. She stopped sauntering back and forth and came to stand very close to Mr. Lawrence. "Please kiss me. I never."

He did. When he unbuttoned Mouse's white nurse's uniform and kissed the large haloes of her nipples, Mouse breathed loudly through her mouth and closed her eyes, holding onto Mr. Lawrence fiercely, as if she were drowning and he were a lifeguard trying to save her. He had to pry her hands off him to unfurl a sleeping bag onto the floor, as Mouse watched deliriously, her eyes drifting, crossed, her fingers hooked into the belt loops of his blue jeans.

After they made love Mouse lay naked on the sleeping bag, her long black hair splayed out above her head like a cloud of coal. When Mr. Lawrence stopped breathing hard he pulled his pants up from his ankles and buttoned his fly. He patted Mouse's hip and told her she should get dressed. She shook her head no and hugged his chest. She wanted to do it again. He said No, not right now.

"Why not?" she asked.

"I have things to do," he said. He had to beg Mouse to get dressed and return to class. Even so Mouse left reluctantly, kissing him over and over again, at the door to the shed, grinning like a contest winner as she walked back to the gym for sixth period physical education class. When Sally Pendergast smacked her in the head while playing volleyball, Mouse didn't even mind.

— — —

On weekdays, Mouse's mother worked for Sebastian Crow and his twin brother, Doug, as a tutor. Sebastian was a child actor whose mother had removed him from the same high school that Mouse attended after he had been nominated for an Oscar as Best Supporting Actor in the film *The Illusion of Being*, about a boy who can see and talk to ghosts. The twins were not identical, Sebastian being the cuter, brighter one. In Dora's estimation he was a thoroughly mediocre student and person but he knew how to emote and he was good at being the center of attention. In this world that counted for something. Plus he had a face that was easy to look at.

Years ago Mouse's mother had received a doctorate in American History at the University of Delaware, but she had also married, had

Mouse, and later divorced. After leaving Mouse's father she applied for a professorship at Montana State, only to be told there were no vacancies. "Plus your Ph.D. is a bit too old," an official told her. She finished her studies twelve years ago and had never taught in her field of expertise? "I don't want to sound judgmental or anything, but by this point in time you might be considered somewhat out of it."

Out of what? Dora asked.

"The loop. The world has changed in the last twelve years," said the official, who would not tell her his name over the phone. "Perhaps you should consider doing something else."

For something else, Dora tutored the children of ranchers and the few rich families who for one reason or another wanted to avoid public school. Any time the students began to dislike her, they could fire her immediately. She had to be nice. She had to coddle them. She worked for an organization called Teachers R Us, an online, for-profit group that specialized in providing tutors for families and children too busy to take the time for ordinary public schools. They boasted a 100% approval rating, a money-back guarantee. Under this system the children were required to write out weekly teacher evaluations. If those went sour, Dora would be canned. She had to smile at the children constantly, like a real estate agent with termites to hide.

After reading only fifteen pages of *The Grapes of Wrath*, Sebastian resented Steinbeck. "Why should I read about a bunch of stupid Okies? What's in it for me?"

Dora gently noted the obvious relevance of the Great Depression.

"I don't like it," said Sebastian. "Can't we read something easier?"

— — —

Mouse promised not to tell anyone. She kept her meetings with Mr. Lawrence in his storeroom secret. She told no one about modeling the nurse uniform for him, of letting him touch her. For almost two months. Until eventually one night at dinner she announced to her mother, "I did it."

"Did what?"

She explained what she and Mr. Lawrence had done in the utility shed. She said she liked it and wanted to do it all the time. She asked if Dora had ever touched a man's Thing. That's what Mr. Lawrence called it.

"After we do it, I want to sleep sleep sleep. But I can't! I have class."

At first Dora planned to tell the school superintendent about Mr. Lawrence, then decided against it. She didn't want anyone to know about Mouse's pregnancy. She told Mouse to stay away from Mr. Lawrence and not to let him touch her anymore. For days Mouse sulked in her room and wouldn't make her bed or pick up her clothes, but she soon forgot about it.

Dora also went to the school one afternoon and spoke with Mr. Lawrence alone. She threatened to tell everyone and prosecute him for rape.

"No, no," he said, shaking his head, his brown plastic hearing aid making him look feeble and decrepit, hardly able to molest anyone. "It wasn't like that at all," he whined.

He agreed not to have any contact with Mouse again.

— — —

When Mouse had her baby Dora did not take her to the hospital. No one was supposed to know. Her mother told her, "This is going to be Our Little Secret." Mouse screamed and breathed hard and the baby came out red and misshapen. Its legs were fused together and covered with shiny, scaly skin, with a thin, leathery, fin-looking appendage at the end, like a beaver's tail. As soon as Mouse saw it she knew what it was. "It's a baby mermaid," she said. "Let's put her in the sea."

Her mother held the baby and tried to pretend that everything was all right. She said, "It's a baby all right."

"It's beautiful," said Mouse. She had never had a baby before! This was the first! "It's the most beautiful baby in the world. Let's name it Baby. Okay? Baby baby baby."

"Oh, Mouse," said her mother.

"Why is your lip doing that?"

Dora's lip was trembling. She shook her head as if she didn't have an answer for the question.

"Tell it to stop, Mama. Stop that, Lip. Stop."

—  —  —

For several days after giving birth Mouse slept almost continuously, only waking to complain of hunger. When she stirred from the softly padded depths of her recovery sleep, surfacing as if from another, better dream world to consciousness in this rough one, her eyes seemed more crossed than ever. Dora fed her bowls of Spaghetti-Os and Campbell's Cream of Mushroom soup. She watched Mouse eat, heard her slurp happily, grow quickly weary, close her eyes, and once again slip into sleep. The walls of Mouse's room were covered with wallpaper whose pattern depicted black quarter horses and palominos in the field of a country farm, with a paddle-wheel mill in the background, turned by a bucolic stream. The air had the salty aroma from the bowls of soup.

Dora sat in Mouse's room, surrounded by these horses, engulfed in the smell of soup, and watched her daughter sleep. She watched Mouse's large, handsome face propped peacefully on the pillows; she watched as a fly lit upon Mouse's forehead and she frowned and twitched her lips.

The first day Dora worried about Mouse, worried she could become infected or continue bleeding. What if Mouse hemorrhaged and she had to explain the birth to a doctor, a hospital, a bureaucrat?

By the second day her body seemed to be recovering. Sleep made her stronger. As she leaned forward to remove the tray that held the bowl of soup and crackers, a tray that straddled Mouse's lap, Dora could feel the strength in Mouse's breath, breath that smelled of onions and cheddar cheese. Even the mushed cracker gunk caught in her large, crooked teeth seemed to reek of a robust and indefatigable spirit.

While Mouse was recovering, Dora kept Baby out of her sight. She bundled up the deformed child and sequestered it in a bassinet in the basement, holding it in her arms and feeding it from a plastic bottle. In the silent coolness of the basement, she inspected the child's deformities. Surely it would never be able to walk. Its legs were fused together, like toes grown close and connected by a fleshy lobe. The fused legs ended in that wide, thin appendage more like a goose's webbed foot than a human's. It could never walk and its brain was most likely feeble and simple.

— — —

On the third day after Baby's birth, Mouse ate a bowl of Tomato soup with Saltine and Ritz crackers, burped, and fell into a deep sleep. Dora bundled up the baby in a blanket and put her in the front seat of the car. The child smelled musky: of formula and talcum powder. Dora's breath blew faint puffs in the cool October air. She drove the winding back road to the shore of Lake Salvation. The orange heart-shaped leaves of aspens swirled past her windshield. When she rolled down the window to breathe, the air was filled with a pungent, spicy smell.

At the concession stand, which sold hotdogs and cans of soda, Dora rented a canoe. In the park beside the concession stand a large family was having a picnic. Dora bought a cup of coffee and returned to sit in the car for over an hour, drinking it and feeding the baby surreptitiously. It had not cried or made any noise, but she was afraid it would start.

After the family finished their picnic and drove away, Dora returned to the canoe she had rented, tied to a small dock cluttered with bright orange life jackets. She carried Baby in a small, closed cardboard box.

As she paddled into the center of the small lake, fog drifted down the hillsides, the wooded slopes of Spotted Bear Mountain, which loomed above the lake. As the fog drifted onto the dark water, it distorted the white trunks and orange leaves of the aspens.

Dora kept paddling, now and then glancing at the box that held Baby, placed carefully in the bottom of the canoe. When water from the paddle spotted the brown, rippled surface of the cardboard, she paddled more slowly, careful to keep any wetness from touching it again.

Soon the fog swallowed her. The white air swirled over the dark, calm waters of Lake Salvation. Dora stopped paddling and, for a few minutes, let the canoe drift.

Out of the fog flew a flock of Canada geese. A pair of loons surfaced near Dora's canoe, the black-and-white feathers of their backs and wings reminding her of a chessboard from her father's old study in a house she'd lived in years ago. Startled by her motion, they beat their wings and took flight, their feet trailing across the surface as they vanished into the whiteness, creating dual wakes in the shapes of long, wet vees.

Finally Dora opened the cardboard box and lifted out the now awakened child. She began to fix an old bicycle chain and padlock around its waist. Baby squirmed and fidgeted. Dora's hands trembled as she fit the chain around her in two loops, the rusting links looking wrong against the bloated infant belly. Baby's face scrunched up tight, her tiny fingers grabbing at air, her fused legs flopping weakly. Her face turned a deep red, her bunched cheeks and mouth swelling as if she would explode. Then she began to wail. The keening cries belled out over the lake in concentric circles of grief.

Dora quickly hugged Baby to her breast. She kissed her forehead and slid her gently into the lake. In the fraction of a moment before Baby vanished, her eyes seemed to glow, piercing through this new wet world.

The sound of her cries suddenly ceased, replaced only the slosh of water against the canoe's aluminum hull.

Dora sobbed and hugged her sides, rocking the canoe as it drifted. After a while it came to a stop in a tangle of lily pads, in the shallows, where tree stumps jutted up from the murk and a swan flew through the white sky, white on white, materializing indistinctly, as if being born from nothing and returning to nowhere.

—   —   —

It was dark by the time Dora returned the canoe. The woman in the concession stand said, "For a minute there I was worried. Thought I was going to have to sick the law on you," she said drily, then winked.

Back in her car, Dora turned on the headlights and returned home, her eyes red and puffy, her nose running. When Dora peeked inside the room with the horse wallpaper, Mouse woke and asked for more soup.

—   —   —

The week after she dropped Baby into the lake, Dora gave Sebastian and Doug a pop quiz on astronomy. Even before she handed out the thirty multiple-choice questions, which Doug always referred to as "multiple-guess," she was ashamed of how easy it was. She had reduced the questions to what she considered was a fifth-grade level, and this was supposed to be a ninth-grade exam. One of the questions asked, "Saturn is the _____ planet from the sun: a) third; b) fifth; c) second; d) sixth."

After a few minutes Sebastian raised his hand. "This test isn't fair. We haven't studied any of this material yet."

Doug looked up and asked, "What does 'elliptical' mean?"

Dora said all of the questions came directly from chapters one and two of the textbook, which she had assigned to them last week.

"I read it last week. But I don't remember any of it," said Doug, and laughed.

"I thought that was due next week," said Sebastian. "I'm not taking a test that isn't fair." He crumpled up his test sheet and tossed it toward the trashcan in the corner of the room, where it bounced off the rim and landed on the floor.

Dora picked up the crumpled paper and unfolded it, smoothing it out on her desk top with her trembling hands. "I've already dumbed down this material far enough. Any lower and I'll be teaching the alphabet again."

"Are you calling us dumb?" asked Sebastian.

Doug grinned. "If we're so dumb, why do we make the big bucks and you're stuck here playing 'Little House on the Prairie'?"

"Yeah," said Sebastian. "What about that, Lady Know-It-All?"

"Pearls before swine," said Dora.

— — —

At the end of the week the boys had fun writing their teaching evaluations. One question on the prepared form asked, "Has this been a rewarding educational experience?" Doug wrote, "Absolutely not! It's been a total waste of my precious time." Another question asked, "Is your tutor well-equipped emotionally and intellectually to instruct?" Sebastian wrote, "She thinks she knows everything but she doesn't. She hates us and she hates herself. If you don't love yourself you can't love anyone else. She needs therapy, big time."

Over the weekend, Mrs. Crow e-mailed Dora that due to these low teaching evaluations, they would no longer need her tutoring services. "P.S.," she added. "I agree with the boys. I think you need professional help."

—  —  —

Dora applied for unemployment and food stamps. She read the classified ads and watched soap operas, lying on the couch and eating microwaved popcorn. During a commercial break on "One Life to Live" Sebastian Crow appeared on the TV screen, acting in a commercial that had been filmed four years ago. He starred as an adorable child with an upset stomach cured by an antacid. His last line in the commercial was, "Thanks, Mom! I feel like a million bucks!"

—  —  —

One day the school called and informed Dora that Mouse had suffered a nosebleed and could she please come and pick her up? When she arrived at the school Dora was directed to the infirmary. In front of the school nurse Mouse said, "I want to see Baby. Where's Baby? I want Baby."

Mouse took the tissue away from her nose as she stared, her mouth hanging open, and in the moment that Dora stared at her, unsure how to answer, a dark ooze of blood appeared at the bottom of her nostrils and began to flow onto her upper lip. Her nipples were also leaking milk, although Dora had dressed her in clothes to conceal this.

—  —  —

On the drive to Lake Salvation, Dora had Mouse fold her seat back and lean her head backwards to staunch the flow from the nosebleed. She had Mouse stuff fresh wads of Kleenex in her nostrils. When the radio happened to play a song Mouse liked, she sang along in a high, nasally voice, sometimes garbling the words unintelligibly. Now and then Dora reached over to pat her leg. Along the roadside the spruce and pine were a deep green, almost black. The sky was solid white with clouds.

Before they reached the lake Mouse put her seat upright and began cooing at the forests and stream that ran alongside the road. Just above the lakeshore, they stopped at a scenic overlook. Mouse rolled down her window and stuck her head out, the wind blowing her hair back wildly. She looked over at Dora and said, "Pretty view! Pretty view!"

The scenic overlook was perched on a cliff above the lake. Tourists headed north to Glacier National Park often pulled over to take photographs there. On one end of the parking lot was an educational placard. It depicted clouds over the lake and its marshy borders, an illustration of Spotted Bear Mountain in the background. The legend on the placard read WHAT HAPPENS TO RAIN? It described how evaporation off the lake joined water vapor and dust particles trapped in clouds too heavy to rise above the mountains that dropped the moisture back onto the mountainside, where it flowed in creaks and streamlets back into the lake: "Rain falls to fill the lake. Water on the lake surface evaporates into the air to fill the clouds. They then grow heavy with water vapor, which falls back to the lake surface as rain. The process is one of constant renewal."

Mouse made Dora read the sign aloud. An older couple who arrived on motorcycles with sidecars stared at her oddly as Mouse repeated Dora's words in her own loud, lisping voice. The man turned to the woman and gave her a quizzical look. A large raven flapped up and landed in the parking lot, pecking at a bag of potato chips scattered on the gray asphalt.

"Let's go down to the lake now," said Dora. She took Mouse by the hand and led her back to the car. The wind was chilly, swirling Mouse's coal-black hair into her face, several threads of it getting caught in her mouth. As they walked past it, the huge raven leapt up and banked into a stiff gust, swinging its dull black body into the sky above the water.

As they were getting into the car, Mouse asked, "We see Baby now?"

Dora started the engine. She said, "I'm going to show you where she is."

— — —

The lower parking lot, near the lakeshore, was weedy and unkempt. In it were only two pickup trucks and a large white RV. Near the water's edge an old man and woman sat in folding chairs, fishing.

Mouse immediately got out and ran toward a flock of Canada geese grouped near the water's edge, in a marshy area full of high grass and cattails. The geese flew away when she neared them, landing in unison again on the lake's surface about fifty yards from shore. Dora followed Mouse, catching up to her at the south shoreline, where a thin strip of pebbly beach mingled with the swampy marsh grass littered with waterlogged sticks, branches, and dark, tubular goose droppings.

"Where's Baby?" asked Mouse. She looked directly at Dora, smiling, the focus of her eyes only slightly off kilter.

Dora told her that Baby was in the lake.

"How did she get there?"

"I put her there."

"How?"

"I rowed a canoe out into the lake and put her in the water."

Mouse smiled and gazed toward the wide expanse of dark blue water, the lake surface scalloped with wind-driven waves, white-capped and mesmerizing. Her nose was running, still slightly bleeding, a thin line of pink snot dribbling to the top of her lip. Dora fished out a Kleenex from her purse and told Mouse to wipe herself off. She didn't want to be a mess, did she?

Mouse ignored her. She started walking away. She said, "I want to see Baby."

Dora followed several steps behind her. Her face shattered into a dozen red pieces.

For a while they walked along the marshy shoreline, getting their shoes covered in mud, their pants legs soggy. Then Mouse cried out, "There she is! There's Baby!"

A trumpeter swan sat on the pebbly shore, its long, sinuous neck curled into a tight S shape. The huge white bird seemed oblivious to Mouse's approach until she was close.

"Baby?" she called. "Baby!"

Finally the swan flew off, beating its wide white wings, holding its long neck and head stretched aloft, its black webbed feet trailing across the wave-rippled surface of the lake. Mouse turned to her mother and asked if she saw it, if she saw Baby, and Dora said Yes, yes, of course she did. She was so different now, yes? She had grown up. She had become so beautiful.

# That Night at the Café

That night at the Café du Coeur there was some discussion about whether the moon was full or not. It was close but perhaps not quite. One of the Americans was said to have checked the calendar and to have announced that it would not be full until the day after next, but for others it was not a matter of calendars and lunar cycles, rather, it was a matter of beauty and a sense of closure. When it came to pass that among the party of fourteen souls, one of them was to die tragically before the eyes, lips, and hands of the others, for all intents and purposes it was later decided that *la lune* had reached the peak of its waxing, at least metaphorically, if not astronomically. It was the kind of moon to which one howls. The aluminum sheen it cast upon that village in southern France was the kind of lyrical and searing light that defines mortal character, revealing both dignity and denial.

In the beginning of that week, when a dozen of the Americans arrived from wherever they had been—all over the world—the moon was a fat sliver of Pushkin hanging in the sky. They had come to learn how to write, though some of them believed it couldn't be taught. Still, this was the south of France. The skeptics could suspend their disbelief for one part literary chitchat and two parts fun in the sun. Besides, we all need a hand to guide us through the darkness of creative night, yes? Words of wisdom never hurt. Pithy quips such as "Show, don't tell." To be placed upon a shelf beside "You are what you eat." And by the second day it was widely agreed, "Whatever you do, never write about writers."

The smoking contingent—banished, as it were, to the devil-may-care risk of premature death and the dusky charm of tobacco—first noticed the waxing moon. They sat at wobbly wooden tables in the middle of the narrow cobblestoned rue de la Mairie, trying to level them by placing matchbooks under the short legs. Neil, a twenty-year-old Dartmouth student, fumbled dazedly with his Gauloises. He'd smoked hashish with a French stranger on the train from Toulouse, and soon after sitting down at the table, spilled wine on his white shirt. But being still stoned, he simply smiled and dabbed ineffectually at the red splotches with a paper napkin.

Mark the unknown novelist and Daniel the wistful father, old friends from years ago in New York, were respectively smoking a Cuban cigar and a pipe. Mark had given up cigarettes six years before, but loved the taste and feel of smoke in his mouth. As far as cigars were concerned, he told himself that you can't get cancer from two or three a month, can you? A few years after quitting cigarettes he also quit his wife. He now enjoyed women as he enjoyed the cigars, fooling himself into thinking that two or three a year couldn't hurt, could they?

Daniel was married with children, two young sons whom he loved more than anything he'd ever known. About his wife he was less certain. He was chafing at domesticity. He couldn't help but feel as if he'd not only mortgaged his house—a comfortable and expensive five-bedroom Swiss minichalet on a hillside overlooking Lake Geneva—he'd also mortgaged his talent and dreams. During the six years since Willie-Bo had been born he'd sacrificed his own dreams of becoming the next Paul Bowles and settled for the joys and sorrows of John Cheever's alter ego, the one who never published, the one without the *New Yorker* credits.

He was a good man who had been raised first in Africa then in Connecticut. His father had been a missionary doctor in the Congo. Daniel rarely spoke of this, but that tradition of sacrifice and devotion to others added to his physiognomy an aura of goodness. He was the kind of person on whom you could rely. In a pinch, he'd be there to help. If need be, he'd take a bullet for the best. It was obvious. People liked him for this quality. You could call it a sense of duty, but that sounds too Kiplingesque, though he did have an air of Tennyson about him, that "Charge of the Light Brigade" quality of doomed honor. His goodness was not righteousness, but rightness. He smoked the pipe, and like his moral probity, it gave off an aroma people liked.

Those first few days, when he was often seen smoking at a wooden table in that narrow cobblestoned street, Daniel had an air of pensiveness about him, a distracted quality that bordered on remoteness. Yet when he puffed on his pipe, his knees spread wide, leaning forward to listen to one of Mark's rambling stories, you got a sense that not only was he listening, but his mind was moving between that and many moments and movements of his past as well. He was a tall and gentle man who had grown a goatee and had gained thirty pounds since Mark had last seen him in New York, but who carried this weight well, the same way he carried his sturdy Yankee goodness.

Mark was the opposite: Since they had last seen each other, ten years before, he had shaved his mustache and lost thirty pounds. In the interval, Daniel had gotten married and Mark had gotten divorced. Daniel's life was one of wistful contentment, something he found troubling, while Mark's life was dominated by anxious hunger—sexual, intellectual, emotional—an adventure that boiled down to troubled searching. Where Daniel bumped against the borders of his life, Mark groped in a void. Each envied the other. Mark wanted Daniel's egg-like completeness (the wife, the children, the sense of being centered) just as Daniel wanted the contents of Mark's psychic duffel bag (the tattooed lovers, the drunken laughter, that sense of risk and thrill).

That first evening, after a rich dinner and many glasses of wine, they both agreed it was a gorgeous night for a smoke, the waxing moon swelling with a sense of greatness and, with the mystery of unknown women in their presence, an inkling of romance.

— — —

Although it was suggested early on that storytellers should "Choose a point of view and stick to it," the women tended to think this a bit autocratic. Winny, in particular, opined that it "reeked of patriarchal mumbo-jumbo." Her husband was a man of firm convictions. He kept a keen eye on the power struggles and political agendas that swirled through the history department at the University of North Carolina-Wilmington, of which he had once been the chair but was now playing a more peripheral role. "More like an Ottoman"—he would quip—"after the empire." Winny loved the man, but at times admitted that she felt a bit intimidated by his tendency to play the know-it-all. She and her best friend, another faculty wife, rebelled quietly, together recognizing their husbands as relics of an old-fashioned, Dead White European Male view of things. "History is exactly the way he looks at it. *His* story."

While Winny attempted to grasp the many, various, and convincing arguments, her husband took the bull by the horns and defeated his opponents, like a paunchy, balding matador with logic as his sword. In a recent short story, Winny had described the death of an Algerian boy, intrigued by the struggle to imagine reality from his quite separate personal background, identity, and frame of perception. Her husband thought the attempt doomed from the outset, doomed by its fuzzy conception, but he held his tongue.

He gave her support. The world was hard enough. He knew there was no sense in emotional sabotage. But he wasn't present the morning when her story was discussed among the group of writers. That morning in the garden, as flowers fell into their laps from the trees above, as Mark chucked pebbles at Daniel's shoes and Neil doodled drawings in his notebook, Winny's husband wasn't there to hear what was said. He wasn't there to hear the discussion of her story, how much the group of writers and readers honestly liked it, what a triumph they thought it to be.

Rain thought it the best story of the week, admiring how Winny had transcended the limits of her self via the imagination. She was a seventeen-year-old prep school student who wore her hair in dreadlocks and loved horses. Overhearing Winny describe her husband, she winced: She believed that the female mind, heart, and figure were superior to the male, and considered marriage mainly a male construct to enforce control.

Although Claire was thirty years younger than Winny, she too struggled in the bounds of a strong husband. Hers was an adventure traveler who, while she was in France, was leading a group of paid customers on a climb of Aconcagua, the highest mountain in the Andes. At first she'd been wowed by his rugged charm and that whole Bruce Chatwin aura, but after two years of marriage she'd learned too well the downside of having a husband who was never home. She noticed she was starting to overlook more than little things: Though she told the group a thrilling tale of rescuing a girl suffering from pulmonary edema on a Himalayan trek, how she had turned back and hiked down to a lower altitude with her, she kept secret the fact that Craig had let her go alone, choosing to stay with the fit and the hardy. With the romantic attentions and invitations that a lovely young woman naturally receives, she was beginning to wonder if being married to Indiana Jones was worth the loneliness. At times, he seemed to inhabit another world. Her book of stories, *The Best Part of You*, was soon to be published, and he had read none of them.

Claire wasn't the only one with a book on the way: Belinda Zelazny, the organizing force of the group, was a writer whose latest novel—a date-rape courtroom drama titled *Don't Touch Me There*—had already been nominated for a national book award, though it was just hitting the stands. She rushed about that laidback medieval village with an excessive amount of brio, scheduling her day like a workaholic junior studio executive trying to impress the bigwigs in L.A. That she managed to schmooze with virtually everyone at breakfast, run the morning workshop, fork up bon mots during lunch with les amis in the plaza, shop for gifts for her children, call her cousin in Avignon to make plans for next week, hike eight kilometers to the eleventh-century abbey and tour it before meeting with two students for private conferences prior to the 7:30 dinner time was considered more than remarkable—it was downright scary.

She told a convincing story of playing tennis with Philip Roth and thoroughly irritated the less-secure personalities of the group. Lila, who later confessed to having expected a quilt-making, touchy-feely type of domestic goddess—an image conjured from the jacket photo on Belinda's second novel, *Handle with Care*—was shocked to discover Belinda more closely resembled the withering, I-can-crush-you mien of Joyce Carol Oates on a too-busy day of book signing at a B. Dalton's in Des Moines, Iowa.

The dozen writers were meant to be divided neatly in a pair of sixes by Belinda, who had buttonholed her pal Mark for the gig and had admitted to him privately that she had placed all the better eggs in her basket. As it turned out, however, the two groups into which these writers fell had little to do with quality or talent: Belinda's group met in the café's dining room, a salon worthy of Gertrude Stein's living room, the kind of dining room in which you could easily imagine Henry Miller playing footsy with Anaïs Nin or, worse yet, swindling both her and the world into thinking something as slapdash and half-baked as *Tropic of Cancer* worthy of the term *masterpiece*.

Her group tended to favor a slash-and-burn critical method, demanding to know the motivations, dreams, fears, and idiosyncrasies of each other's fictional constructs, with some of them filling the downtime by dropping the names of editors, agents, or publishers as if their very mention would somehow engender monetary success, while the others became justly irritated and stressed out by this too-rich diet of ambition and envy.

Mark's group met in the courtyard of the *mairie* (the mayor's offices), a small arboretum of sorts, where it was kosher to eat the plums from the trees, indulge in lengthy discussions about favorite books and films, and make wisecracks about the silly accents of French sheep. They commented about how they enjoyed the slower, more relaxed pace of life in the south of France, though the term *joie de vivre* was justly banned from everyone's lips and pens, along with *Kafkaesque* and *c'est la vie*.

The weather, as well as the physical details, made them keenly aware of the setting. Wooly worms undulated across fallen darkish leaves, the wind whipped pink oleander blooms into a frenzy, and, as the writers nailed down a list of dos and don'ts—the pathetic fallacy, for instance, was pooh-poohed, summed up by the useful "Avoid ascribing emotions to inanimate objects"—the clouds yawned and, when a scatter of raindrops speckled the loose-leaf notebooks of the group, appeared to be weeping.

— — —

For all the contrary opinions and competing agendas, at first, at least, there was surprisingly little infighting. The setting hypnotized that hodgepodge of writers. In the narrowness of those lovely cobblestoned streets, in the flickering shadows of plane trees in the town plaza, with their Nabokovian piebald trunks as the backdrop, it didn't take long for loyalties and cliques to develop, hearts to be wooed, and confidences to be shared. Mark, Daniel, and Neil comprised the trio of jokers and film freaks, the ones who laughed at everything, saw the world as a vast, ongoing film treatment, and seemed to be having the time of their lives. Monica, Rain, and Claire kvetched about the overzealousness of Belinda's headstrong ways, while Bess, Winny, and Lane deconstructed just what a flagrant flirt Mark was, noting bitterly that you had to be pretty or funny to get his attention. It wasn't fair.

On the other hand, Mark and Daniel encouraged Neil to woo Rain. But as much as she intrigued him, he had to admit that her dreadlocks were a bit *dégoûtant*. Carlo, the Italian Old Master, was loved by everyone, though it didn't stop them from laughing at his quirks. He seemed to have brought a steamer trunk full of the manuscripts of his life's work, and to have dabbled in every literary genre, all available in neatly bound photocopies. To Mark he showed a play that won the prestigious Dolce Vita award in 1983; to Daniel he showed the screenplay that was never filmed, though Federico Fellini was to arrange funding for its production at the time of his death. To Neil, nicknamed Rookie of the Year but whose constant hijinks and overall youthfulness made his judgment somewhat suspect in the Old Master's eyes, he showed a short story he'd written two weeks ago.

Lila, a dreamy and vulnerable thirty-two-year-old Ph.D. student, was thoroughly charmed by Carlo's Italian savoir faire but laughed nervously when he sat across from her at the dinner table and said, "Let us now talk over sex."

— — —

On that third night, Daisy and Iona—the British owners of the café—feted the crew to a "literary recipe" dinner, every recipe being a famous writer's favorite dish. It started out with a Jean-Paul Sartre tossed salad (there was no salad dressing, of course), followed by the George Bernard Shaw vegetarian pie. "Careful with the Oscar Wilde secret sauce," quipped Mark. Dessert honored Marcel Proust's *A la recherche du temps perdu*: madeleine cakes soaked in lime-flower tea. During conversation that night, after it was posited that "One should always avoid the passive voice," a contest was proposed. Everyone's attention was snagged by Mark when he rapped a spoon against his wineglass, then declared that each of them should write a story beginning with the words "That night at the café." A bottle of champagne would be awarded to the winner. During Sunday's dinner at the Ferme Auberge, their last night together, all the stories would be read aloud, from which a winner would be chosen.

After dinner, Daisy shushed the rowdy crowd and implored them to keep their voices down: They were making enough noise to wake the dead! The ragtag group of writers bought three more bottles of wine and walked down to the stone bridge at the edge of town. Perhaps they'd had too much already. Mark and Daniel leapt upon the bridge parapet, which was wide enough to balance upon easily, though on one side there was a two-hundred-foot plunge. Mark proposed they play the drinking game that Prince Andre wins in *War and Peace*, in which the contestants balance on the edge of a windowsill high above a street, grip bottles of wine in their teeth, and without using their hands, tilt the bottles back and drink their entire contents without spilling any and without plunging to their deaths below. Though both of them held out their hands as if they were walking on a tightrope, and both held plastic cups of red wine in their teeth, and both seemed unable to tear their gaze off the huge blue-white moon in the sky above the stony grandeur of Languelieu, Mark thought the parapet almost too wide, too easy, not sporting enough.

Richard, a British fellow who owned a local curio shop and seemed inordinately jealous of other men if his passably attractive wife were anywhere visible, importuned the daredevils to please, please get down from there, you could fall on the stones below and that would be a frightful sight, don't you think? His idea of fun was a bit more reserved than the Americans'. It consisted of making references to the Bloomsbury set while fingering the buttons of his woolen vest and wondering with how many men his wife had been unfaithful to him. He lectured the rowdy writers on the downside of this part of France: The beaches to the south were too crowded in the summer, the narrow streets of Languelieu too windy in winter, and during spring, the migrating geese made a frightful racket. Mark pretended to listen—mentally pegging Richard as the personality type known as British Momma's boy—as he kept an eye on Lila, and perked up when he heard her ask how hard it was to reach the river below: She loved the sound of water in the night. Could she go down and see it? Was there a footpath? Would it be too dark?

Offending Richard by striding away without so much as a by-your-leave, Mark offered to join Lila in a walk to the river. At first Richard scuttled behind them, warning of all the treacherous traps ahead: The rocks were slick, polished too smooth and covered with moss; the sting nettles could send a fair-skinned person to the hospital; and it was believed that bandits sometimes lurked in the shadows below the bridge. With his lips almost touching Lila's ear, Mark whispered, "Yeah right, Nigel. And the dragonflies will as soon as suck your eyeballs out as look at you." She laughed and, knocked off-balance slightly by his nearness, stumbled slightly, so that Mark had to catch her from falling, though perhaps it wasn't absolutely necessary to place both of his warm hands on her waist, letting them linger a few heartbeats after she'd regained her footing.

Though one contingent of the writers argued that "Prose should avoid the earmarks of poetry," it was hard that evening night to surrender to the lyrical charms of the dusky *la nuit*. The path to the river began at the base of the city wall, wound under the stone arches of the bridge (where no bandits lurked), weaved through a mass of trees, leaves, weeds, and nettles (which did smart a bit, but not that badly) to the smooth white and gray limestone boulders in the riverbed below, huge round white stones that resembled those described by García Márquez at the beginning of *One Hundred Years of Solitude* as being like "prehistoric eggs."

Mark and Lila had no flashlights; all they needed was moonlight. When the canopy of trees blocked out that silvery light, they were thrilled to creep on in total darkness, Lila so close upon Mark's back that he could feel the warmth of her sweet breath on his neck. It was brighter down by the water, with a break in the interlocking arms of the tree branches above. The water slipped softly over the boulders, pushing pieces of driftwood against the banks with a susurrus, wet murmur. There were dragonflies in the moist air, though none of them swooped to suck out Mark or Lila's eyes. Here and there, like the surprise glimpse of falling stars, fireflies flashed, marking the night with faint scars of light.

Mark and Lila found the flattest limestone boulder to serve as a park bench. It was covered with patches of dark moss that would stain his blue jeans and her white skirt, but what the heck. He wanted to kiss Lila but instead asked who her favorite authors were. Lila told him that for the last year she had been living in Germany and was out of it as far as the latest American writers were concerned, but most recently she'd been reading British writers. She liked Martin Amis's novels and thought him a terrific writer; Mark liked the earliest books (*The Rachel Papers*, *Dead Babies*, and *Success*, for instance) but thought the latest (*London Fields* and *The Information*) rather inbred.

Lila also liked such women writers as Ellen Gilchrist and Jill Mc-Corkle. As she spoke, she wondered if he were going to kiss her. She wasn't sure whether she wanted that or not, or what it would be like. She was suspicious of succumbing to the European-vacation, writer's-conference fling. That might be cheesy. (Being in France, is the term *fromagey*?) They talked for half an hour and when she yawned sleepily, Mark suggested they head back to the hotel. As they worked their way across the riverbed, having to stretch from stone to stone, Mark held her hand whenever it would help, telling her to keep an eye out for bandits. At one point he dunked his foot in the water and she laughed brightly. Ascending the dark path to the bridge and town, he touched her waist more tenderly than before, his fingertips lingering even longer.

When they returned to the hotel, their ankles and shins were zigzagged with scratches from the stinging nettles. Mark invited Lila into his room and, in the candlelight, rubbed antibiotic ointment onto her skin. She thanked him softly, and as they were about to part, he kissed her lips. In that moment he was too dizzy to think, but later he remembered the German word for soft, *weich*—the initial consonant pronounced like an English *v*, the final two consonants aspirated, wetly "voiced" into a gentle hissing sound. That word somehow defined his thoughts of Lila. Time seemed to move more slowly during the moment in which he rubbed the ointment onto her scratches. There was a tenderness there for which all of us long, and before they blew out the candle and closed each of their doors (she had the room adjacent to his in the hotel above the Café du Coeur), they kissed again, for the sheer sweet touch of it. After the doors were closed and they were safe in bed, each had trouble sleeping.

The next night Lila slept in Mark's bed, though she rose at dawn to steal back to her room, trying not to wake Rain, Winny, or Monica with the impossibly loud snap of the tongue in Mark's door lock.

As the week wore on and more principles were broached—"Avoid clichés" hung on the same rack with "Don't mix your metaphors," while someone later tossed the old bone of "Make your characters round, not flat" into the pot—people made friends along the lines of a mixture of political stances and physical appearances. Fay, a large African-American woman, mother of three children, married to the same man for eighteen years, seconded Winny's opinion about the autocracy of that point-of-view thing, pegging it as "bossy male bullshit." In her thinking, Belinda was borderline wacko, and Mark both arrogant and dim.

A hefty woman who resembled the pre-fitness-crazed Oprah Winfrey, Fay saw no sense in Mark's skinny white-boy song and dance. He lived in a completely different world from her and it showed. Though she was close to finishing her doctorate at the University of New Orleans, she announced at the start her desire to write supermarket best-sellers, and as that baby failed to cry, she could tell she rubbed these academic drones the wrong way. That was okay by her. She could chill with the best of them. Most likely they envied her gutsiness. Not a thing wrong with success. Or ambition. Fay was honest: She wanted to be the next Terry McMillan, but she wasn't going to hold her breath. Her time would come. But while she waited, she didn't see why she had to suffer these bony fools. To her, Belinda looked ill. A body isn't supposed to be that thin. Chicken necks, yes. Not human beings. She liked Winny's girth and presence. There was a woman who didn't spend hours in front of the mirror. There was a woman who knew how to enjoy a good meal, how to raise and love her kids, how to handle the jazz *and* the blues.

For those who weren't staying up till dawn making love, twisting the night away in white cotton French sheets while experiencing a mixture of embarrassment and giddy thrill, there were plenty of other diversions. Some played tennis, others played chess. You could search for gifts in the puppet shop, browse in the handmade paper store, and if the jealous husband of the British lovely were there, make him uncomfortable by asking such questions as "Are your envelopes lickable?" There was horseback riding, bocce ball playing, tarot card reading, not to mention swimming in the two rivers that encircled the *village du livre*.

Friday at noon a party drove in Daniel's Renault to the beach at Leucat, at which Neil made everyone laugh with long renditions of Steven Seagal action scenes. As if defining the maxim that "Action equals character," Belinda the busy novelist kept up her frenzied pace. In the five short days before Friday night's tragedy, she managed to complete three chapters of her next book, *Your Heart or Mine*, negotiate a movie deal with the TNT cable network, get a great bargain on antique cutlery for her cousin's wedding, and arrange a Fulbright fellowship for an upcoming sabbatical leave.

Her breakneck approach to life did have its triumphs. It was Belinda, for instance, who created the framework for Winny to read her novel-in-progress, a secret work completely entwined in her heart.

— — —

That day several of the writers piled into Daniel's Renault and drove to Carcassonne to tour the local castle, nine of them in the small car, Mark making wisecracks and laughing even more than usual, causing Neil to comment, "You're in an awfully good mood today," his romantic suspicions further confirmed when Mark became all smirks upon the suggestion that, to save room, Lila sit in his lap. The castle was a triumph of twelfth-century architecture and twentieth-century tourism. A crowd of British schoolchildren chanted soccer songs while brandishing plastic swords, wearing plastic helmets, and dreaming that one day they too could become marauding hooligans.

Rain bought a ceramic ashtray in the shape of a skull, Daniel and Mark ogled the shopgirls, Bess and Fay couldn't decide on anything to buy, and Lila wondered if Mark would turn out to be a jerk like too many of the others. From the turrets you could see the Pyrenees, the Mediterranean, and happy families who were perhaps too alike videotaping the whole thing in a similar fashion. When the narrow streets echoed with the shrieks and squeals of schoolkids, Mark wryly suggested that perhaps the time had come to enact Dorothy Parker's adage: "Kill your darlings."

Dinner that evening was a grand and stylish affair, a picnic catered by Iona and Daisy, something straight out of Chekhov—*The Duel*, perhaps, with its sturgeon eggs, samovars, and erotic intrigue. They drove the Americans to a hill overlooking the village, to the very crest, with a 360-degree view of the countryside—fields full of gray sheep, yellow sunflowers, green vineyards—all bathed in a dying tangerine light reminiscent of the Tuscany eulogized by Bernardo Bertolucci's *Stealing Beauty*. There were tablecloths spread across the grass of the promontory, near a gap in the pines, from which they could spy the two rivers that encircled and enchanted Languelieu.

To the south, closer to Carcassonne, a hot air balloon in the shape of an elaborate chateau floated like some fantastic offspring of the Swiss hotel in *Tender Is the Night* and the celestial schooner in *The Adventures of Baron Munchausen*. The food was superb. There was baskets of bread, bottles of wine, and an exotic fruit pastry dessert of which Iona refused to divulge the secret recipe. Flies had to be shooed from the wedges of *fromage*.

On a hillside across the valley a ring of cone-shaped trees stood out noticeably. Winny, who lived just an hour and a half away, said it must be a cemetery. She explained that the locals ringed the cemeteries with cypress trees, their vertical graces and uplifted branches suggesting an easy ascent into the heavens. "A lovely thought," she added, before taking another bite of bread and cheese. She ate heartily, though she later expressed an anxiousness about returning to the café to do her reading—nervous, of course, on the eve of her performance. Belinda looked more relaxed than usual, her energies spent by a tennis game earlier in the day in which Neil had spanked her six-two, six-love. The "boys" were off to one side, spastic with laughter and basking in the attention of Rain, who tried hard not to cover her mouth while she laughed because, now that her braces were off, her teeth were really quite lovely.

Their bellies full and the wine bottles empty, the picnickers disbanded and returned to Languelieu anyhow they could. Daisy and Iona packed the baskets and leftovers into the antique black London taxi, a handful of people piled into Daniel's Renault, and the others chose to walk. The moon was big and bright enough to make you believe in whatever we mean when we use the word God. Neil did an imitation of Claire crossing a rope bridge in Nepal, carrying three dying Sherpani children on her shoulders, and she didn't think it was the least bit funny. Mark and Lila lingered far enough behind the others so as to hold hands and smooch without causing tongues to wag.

It was nearly eleven by the time all gathered once again at the Café du Coeur, and Daisy and Iona placed burning candles on the dining room tables to light Winny's reading, to give it a nice golden glow. Someone made a joke about the picnic having a Last Supper feel, and Daniel asked in a mock-solemn voice, "Who will be the one to betray me?" Becoming aware of how late it was and how far off the schedule they were, Belinda directed everyone to be seated. The smoking contingent lounged against the stone wall lining rue de la Mairie, passing the same pink butane lighter between them as they lit up. Winny had already begun reading by the time they straggled in, woozy with wine, the beads of the doorway clicking with disapproval at their tardiness. Mark's Cuban cigar wouldn't fit in the ashtray, so he placed it carefully on the table's edge as he sat down, and when his chair scraped the floor, making a loud, grating sound, Neil frowned histrionically.

Winny's voice was clear and strong, and she smiled as she read this story, a piece of magic from her life. For her, the subject had something of the quality of forbidden moments. She was sixty-three years young and had waited over two thirds of her life to tell this story. That night was her big break, her moment of glory. The passage she read was an excerpt from a novel manuscript, a mixture of roman à clef and coming-of-age saga, and the sound of her voice penetrated the hollows and shadows of that candlelit room as if the listeners were providing the audience for a confession.

With her hair now white and her face flushed bright pink from too much fine food and wine, and her breath slightly labored as her lungs tried to sustain the mass of her body—which had expanded in recent years—it took a flex of the imagination to envision her as the woman in her story: a pretty twenty-year-old girl attending Amherst College in the mid-fifties, carrying on a clandestine and hypnotic love affair with a fellow student who happened to be a black man from Virginia. She described him as a lover who made her feel as she had never felt before.

She had never told her husband about these dizzy moments in her past. She was glad he wasn't there now to hear her. She could never have described making love to another man, being so physically and emotionally thrilled by another man, in front of her husband. It would have been cruel. And she was not a cruel person. She was grateful to have this audience who would not judge, who would most likely find it fascinating and perhaps, even, their estimation of her character and her personality would increase after hearing it. She thanked them before she began.

Once into the telling of the story, as she read aloud descriptions of taking baths with this handsome and thrilling young man, lingering on the smell and feel of his skin, she couldn't help but smile. That smile, and the clarity and power of her voice, captivated the attention of the thirteen people in the room. She had read several pages before she suddenly paused and looked as if she would take a drink from the glass of water beside her on the dining room table.

To those closest to her, with the best view of Winny's face in the golden glow of the candlelight, her face took on an expression curiously dizzy and disoriented. She tried to take a sip of water, but that simple effort seemed to take a great deal of difficulty; her hand appeared to be moving in slow motion or within a pool of invisible mud, and her fingers pushed dumbly against the glass, knocking it over. "Oh, my," she said, and started to slump.

The women closest to her, Rain and Monica, rushed to hold her body, calling her name, but she could only gasp for breath. As everyone stepped in close to try to help, Mark reminded Claire he knew how to give CPR and he could help her out. Earlier in the week Claire had read a story about taking a class in CPR training, and the two of them had discussed it afterward. People tried to hold Winny's head up and give her a freshly filled glass of water to drink, but her breath rattled. Catching a glimpse of her eyes rolled back in their sockets, Daniel and Mark struggled to lower her heavy body to the ground, Claire cradling her head.

Monica, who was sharing a double room with her, told them Winny was on medication for high blood pressure. She went upstairs to search Winny's things for the prescription bottle. Mark and Claire felt for a pulse in the clammy skin of her neck and the veins of her limp wrist. Fay couldn't stand to watch, so, unnoticed in the hubbub, she went up to her room and curled into a ball. Even then she believed Winny was already dead. She had seen this before. People were always dying around her. She wondered if it were something about her. She felt herself to be a vortex of death, an involuntary, uncontrollable force dragging others toward a crisis. She knew perfectly well what others would have said about the tragedies she'd been fated to behold. She knew they would have told her it was nonsense, that she was in no way to blame for her uncle's electrocution, her landlord's fall from the roof, the motorcycle accident in Morocco, the burning children in Uganda. . . . All of it was mere coincidence, right?

And now this. It meant nothing of course. There was not a pattern here. It was just random chance. Dumb luck. Bad luck. That she had remained physically unscathed in all of these instances meant nothing. She was not intact. She curled more tightly into a ball, sobbing, her face twisted in pain; she prayed for Winny's soul.

In the dining room below, the crowd of writers watched in anguish as Daniel, Claire, and Mark tried to save Winny's life. They could find no pulse. Mark felt something like a heartbeat in her wrist, but feared it was his own frantic muscle insisting it would continue on no matter what. They pulled up her shirt to reveal her belly, pale and enormous. She no longer seemed to be struggling to breathe, though her lips moved slightly with gasps. Mark put his ear on her chest and heard the sound of nothing. That did it. He started pushing down on the center of her chest in one-second intervals, counting aloud "One one-thousand, two one-thousand," in a frantic and desperate voice, until he reached five one-thousand, at which point Claire would blow breath into Winny's mouth.

They smelled the rancid tang of vomit on Winny's lips and turned her over to try to flush it out of her mouth and onto the floor. A splatter of brown slime dribbled from her mouth as Mark pried open her jaw to allow it to leak free, immediately grabbing the paper towels that someone handed to him to absorb it. With another paper towel he wiped Winny's mouth before Claire blew in another breath. When Mark started pumping on Winny's chest again, Claire said, "I don't know if I'm getting any air to her. She might be choking on her own vomit." Mark told her not to worry. He could see her lungs rising up. He told Claire she was doing a great job. Winny was not going to die. They were not going to let her.

"Come on, Winny," he pleaded. "You're not going to die. You've got things to do tomorrow. It's not time to go yet." At one point he was close to breaking down in tears and instead shouted at the other people in the room, the people behind them, watching, the ones he couldn't see; he shouted at them to help, goddamnit! They needed some help! They needed support! "Where are the fucking EMS people?" he shouted.

"They're coming," said Claire. "Don't get angry. They'll be here as soon as they can."

— — —

And then, for a moment, Winny seemed to revive. Or seemed to be giving them hope of the possibility that she might revive. In a pause between Mark's pumps on her heart and Claire's breath filling her lungs, Winny's lips moved and she gasped. Mark and Claire urged her on. "Come on, Winny! Breathe! You can do it! Come back to us! It's not time to leave yet!"

Winny took a loud, wet breath, with a liquidy sound in her throat. "Look!" Mark shouted. "She's breathing! She's not going to die!"

They froze for a moment, suspended in the hope that they might have saved her. Winny's eyes were still rolled up, showing too much cornea, and her face was ashen and pale, but her lips were still pink. Mark's voice was loud and desperate as he insisted she was not going to die, she was going to live. All of this—these hopes, all of their hopes, all of the desperate yearning to bring this woman out of her coma and back into the land of the living—collapsed when she took another struggling, phlegmy wet breath, and then stopped. That was death. Mark had never seen it before. Still, he recognized it immediately. "Oh, God," he said. "She stopped breathing. Let's go."

He leaned over her once again and began pumping down on her chest. After five pumps he paused and Claire pushed breath into her lungs. They repeated this a few times and again Winny seemed to revive. Again she struggled to breathe. With less hope than before they watched as the same pattern was repeated. She took two rattling wet breaths and then stopped. Again they began pumping down on her chest and filling her lungs with breath, but after the second pair of wet breaths, she no longer seemed to be reviving. She was slipping away. More food came up from her stomach and they turned her on her side, Claire holding up her head and Mark trying to wipe the vomit off her mouth. To relieve Claire, Mark took over blowing air into Winny's lungs for a moment, but the taste of vomit on her lips made him retch, and though he tried to blow breath into her lungs powerfully, he felt it was only getting in her mouth.

It was almost half an hour before a local doctor arrived. He was a small, dark-haired feckless man who carried none of the sense of authority or confidence that is expected of doctors, but approached Winny's body rather hesitantly and cautiously. He seemed very much the nineteen nineties version of a small-town Charles Bovary. Claire and Mark continued their efforts at resuscitation as the doctor vaguely poked and prodded at Winny's body, until the EMS team, two women and a man, arrived.

They took over hesitantly. They spoke in soft voices and wore pale blue jackets, like lab smocks. They seemed to ignore the doctor as they rigged up a heart monitor to Winny's chest, working with less of a sense of urgency than had Mark and Claire. They inserted a plastic tube into her throat and blew air into her lungs by compressing a black rubber balloon connected to the plastic tube. Mark sat on a chair looking over Winny and the medics. The male EMS person took over pumping Winny's chest, but he seemed to be doing it too softly. All of the Americans kept waiting for the medics to use the electric paddles they had seen revive heart attack victims so often on TV. It didn't happen. They later learned that French EMS teams don't have that technology.

Mark watched the heart monitor machine as Claire spoke to the EMS women in French. He couldn't understand what was being said, but he could tell by their tone of voice that it was not good. The pace of activity lost its frenzy. Claire suggested that they talk to Winny, and she and Mark urged Winny to hang on, don't give up, you're going to make it, your time is not up yet, you've got things to do tomorrow, you have stories left to write, your children need you, your husband needs you, don't leave us, Winny, we all want you back. Their voices pleaded, urged, cajoled. Mark wasn't giving up. He started to tell Claire of a mountain climbing accident he knew about, in which a man was struck by lightning and people had worked on him for half an hour before he revived, but Claire asked him to stop. She couldn't think about that right now. The feckless doctor faded into the shadows. Daisy came over to sit beside Mark and Claire. She asked why they didn't shock Winny with the paddles. The EMS women spoke amongst themselves in low voices.

When the man quit pumping down on Winny's chest, the lines on the heart monitor went flat. They quit moving. Everything stopped. Finally one of the women reached over and turned off the machine.

Mark folded his arms and put his face into them, smashing his forehead against the hard bones. His abdomen began to quake with sobs. The room was quiet but for the sounds of weeping and the faint, soft French voices of the EMS team. Someone placed a table-cloth over Winny's body. Belinda recited the twenty-third psalm. The living wept, pulling their bodies close to each other to feel something, to feel the warm mystery of their still-beating hearts.

As Mark struggled to choke back his tears, he suddenly rose from his crumpled position in the chair and left the dining room of the café, rushing down the rue de la Mairie to escape the condolences, the bonding, the voices, the weeping—all of it. He sobbed as he rushed down the darkened streets of the village, keeping his head down so that the few people he passed couldn't see his face con-vulsed by grief and anguish, the sense of having failed at something worthwhile. He rushed weeping through the streets before reach-ing the bridge at the edge of town. He then climbed down into the darkness, to the river below. There he split the night air with a scream. All the muscles in his body were spasmodically tense. He curled into a ball on the limestone boulder and wept for Win-ny's soul and his own. He recited the Lord's prayer aloud, though he worried over the hypocrisy of this act of contrition. He'd been raised a Catholic but no longer believed. Part of him wanted to, but he couldn't. Curled in a ball on the mossy-smelling limestone boulder, his mind returned to the nonsensical French phrase he'd picked up from the dictionary not long before he left for Europe: *Mettez vos livres plus bas.*

Under the stone archways of the bridge, with the smell of wet leaves, damp sand, and moss in the air, its breath enveloping him in the cool darkness, the sound of the river started to soothe him, remind him: Life is a river, after all. Every last one of us will some-day disappear into the ocean night. It was then that he grasped the meaning of that cryptic phrase found by chance (which doesn't ex-ist): *Mettez vos livres plus bas.* "Put your books lower down." All is vanity. Pride is one of the seven deadly sins. The love of literature is what's important, the magic of art, that link of imagination that connects one person's mind to another, opening your eyes to the beauty and terror of this world. The godlike joy of creation. All of that has nothing to do with book contracts, talk shows, advances, royalties, and movie deals. *Put your books lower down.* Open your eyes to the wonder of this life, this chance, this swing at bat. Before it's gone. Before all you have left is the hollow tang of ambition. This too shall pass. You too shall some day lie motionless and lifeless on a café floor, the ripples of your existence, of your ex-presence, spread-ing outward like the vibration of your energy fading softly into the murk of infinity.

After Mark calmed down, after being curled on the limestone boulder for most of an hour, he stood up, stretched his muscles, then took his shirt off and washed it clean of Winny's vomit. The moon was very bright and the night air felt warm as he knotted the shirt around his waist and walked slowly back to the café. Daniel, who was driving the streets of Languelieu in his Renault, spotted him on the road and pulled over. He'd been looking for him. Daniel got out of the car and they hugged in the headlights. When he asked Mark if he was okay, Mark nodded and said it was really a beautiful night, the moon being so full and everything.

He asked Daniel if he wanted to have a smoke and walk around the village, and Daniel said yes, that would be a good thing. They returned to the café to drop off the car. Mark had to get a clean shirt from his hotel room and was quietly shocked when he saw that Winny's body still lay on the dining room floor, covered by the wine-spotted tablecloth. By French law and custom, it could not be moved until examined by the coroner, until all the paperwork had been filled out, the death certificate signed, everything properly validated. It was several hours before this was accomplished. All of that time her body lay there with an almost vulgar ordinariness, as if she had been the victim of a Mafia assassination and not a woman with dignity and poise.

Earlier in the week, while having lunch at the Café Floreal, beneath the branches of the plane trees in the plaza, the group had discussed the parallels between contemporary and classical literature. Mark compared *Antigone* to Raymond Carver's short story, "So Much Water So Close to Home"—the burial-of-the-dead motif. The idea that how we treat the dead defines and in some ways illuminates how we treat the living. Antigone is in anguish because she wants to bury her brother, Polynices, rather than allow his body to be ripped apart by wild dogs beyond the gates of the city. She must beg King Creon for justice. In Carver's story a group of fishermen in a western state of the U.S. find a girl's nude body floating in the river on the first day of a three-day fishing trip, and rather than hike back the five miles to tell the authorities, they continue on with their fishing, wrapping a loop of fishing line around her finger to keep the body from floating away. They also spend the time getting drunk and washing their camping pots and pans in the water near her body. When they report their find to the police, it turns out she had been raped and killed, and the townspeople are horrified they could be so callous as to leave her body in the water that weekend and continue on with their "fun."

—  —  —

Saturday morning had all the symptoms of aftermath. The living slept late and later struggled down to a breakfast of stale croissants and lukewarm coffee. Daniel and Claire were giddy with exhaustion and nervous tension, having left to pick up Winny's husband in a small town outside Toulouse at four o'clock in the morning, getting lost several times, driving through eerie fog in which the mottled bodies of Languedoc cows would suddenly loom huge and frightening in the ditches beside the road, and, as the dim light of dawn turned the fog into a whiter mist, huge black crows replaced the cows, flapping heavily away from the carcasses of dead rodents on which they had been feeding until the headlights of Daniel's Renault flashed upon their iridescent black wings.

They rolled through sleeping villages full of cats and glowing bluish streetlamps; it took them over four hours to reach the town, and only an hour and a half to return. Winny's husband, Frank, was a bald man with deeply tanned skin and deeply bloodshot eyes behind a large pair of gray-framed glasses. No one knew what to say to him. He would seem well composed for a while, then break into tears. What do you say? How do you speak? There are no words. Some of them hugged him. Others shook his hand.

In the early afternoon, Belinda took charge. Though all the hotels in town were filled for the night, she shuffled people from one room to the next, and made accommodations for Frank and one of Winny's daughters, Karen, who had been living in Grenoble, teaching at a university there. It was regrettable, but Rain agreed to sleep in Winny's bed. Monica shouldn't have to stay in the room alone, anyway. After lunch, Belinda called the group together for an organizational meeting. She announced that due to the present circumstances, class would be canceled for the day, though they would convene tomorrow morning, about ten or so, for the final workshop.

That night there was to be the Festival of St. John, a midsummer fertility ritual in which they would torch a bonfire, burn a scarecrow effigy, drink wine, eat sausage, dance, and when the fire finally burned down, the young boys of the village would be urged to leap over the heap of embers as a sign of their virility. Sunday night would go as planned, with an elaborate dinner at the local Ferme Auberge, a restaurant/inn in which all of the food served was grown on the farm, completely fresh. Their specialty was cassoulet, a sausage-and-beans dish considered one of the defining local flavors. It had to be ordered days in advance. This had all been discussed earlier in the week. Winny had been one of the group to order the cassoulet.

Belinda explained that since Winny would not be present for the dinner on Sunday night, there was an extra dish of cassoulet if anyone was interested. While she was speaking, Mark watched Lila's face, and at the comment about the extra dish of cassoulet being available Sunday night, she winced as if someone had twisted her hand. Later in the afternoon, when Belinda wasn't around, the others expressed outrage. They couldn't believe she would say such a thing!

"What does she want us to do after that?" asked Fay. "Split her dessert?"

— — —

Among the writers who attended the Festival of St. John that night, the atmosphere resembled the remorse and moral hangover at the end of Hemingway's *The Sun Also Rises*, after Lady Brett has slept with the young matador and Robert Cohn has beaten him in a jealous fit, when Montoya looks on the American and British so-called aficionados of the Pamplona festival with scorn and disapproval, because they have shown a lack of respect and dignity for tradition, for the mythical "smell of death," which Hemingway was to write about much more so, years later, in *For Whom the Bell Tolls*.

At the festival, there was much wine drunk, sausage and cheese eaten. Since the previous year's bonfire had caught some trees aflame and threatened to consume the village, this year's blaze was more modest: a four-foot high cone of fallen wood and logs positioned in front of the clay tennis courts. Pine trees waved in the wind fifty yards beyond the fire, and a rather drunken member of the local volunteer fire department sprayed sporadically at the embers that floated toward the wall of evergreen boughs. The French children of the village sang and danced in a circle around the flames. Neil, the youngest male of the Americans, leapt over the embers when the flames were still fairly high.

— — —

According to the calendar that Belinda had consulted earlier in the week, the moon would reach its zenith Sunday night, and true to form, that evening, in the sky over southern France, it rose orange and huge, low on the horizon. It was visible through the trees surrounding the patio dining area of the Ferme Auberge, where the group of thirteen American writers gathered for a last supper. The air smelled of smoke from the wood smoldering in a fire pit, above which hung two legs of lamb. Young chickens pecked at seeds and crumbs at the foot of the dining table, scampering away quickly when Daniel tried to tweak their feathers. The stress of Winny's death took a toll on the writers' spirits.

Belinda and Bess had words over the organization of the writers' workshop; Bess offering the opinion that Belinda misjudged and wrongfully de-emphasized the hazards of such an undertaking, causing Belinda to suggest that perhaps next year Bess could organize her own group, but until then to please keep her comments to herself. Daniel and Mark clashed when Mark's feelings became hurt, thinking that Daniel had laughed at a poem Mark had shown to him, Mark then getting back at Daniel by implying he was something of a literary oaf. (At the end of dinner both apologized to each other for being rude and insensitive, hugging drunkenly in the restaurant's driveway.) Neil, Monica, and Fay chose to leave early, which put Belinda into further fits of ill humor. Claire argued in French with the sarcastic and harried waitress, calling her a "shit," while Carlo urged Mark to tell a story about one of his ex-sweethearts eulogized in the poem Daniel was accused of ridiculing, all of which hurt Lila's feelings, being, as it were, Mark's current sweetheart and not interested in becoming the object of future poems, ridicule, and drunken banter.

Belinda caught a taxi back to the village before dessert was served to organize the final event of the writers' extravaganza week: a reading in French staged before the entire village. With most of the crowd still at the Ferme Auberge drinking wine and waiting on a dessert of muscatel grapes that seemed to be taking as long to prepare as a chapter of *Madame Bovary*, it was less than a total success. Villagers came and sat on the periphery of the dining room of the Café du Coeur, watched stonily as Belinda read from her latest novel in a slapdash, bad French translation—accompanied by its bad French pronunciation—and left, making gestures to each other that summed up the absurdity of the event.

Daisy and Iona felt betrayed by the group as they had donned their finest dresses and done their hair especially for the evening, had placed candles throughout the room to give it a mystical and golden glow—perhaps, in part, to dispel the aroma of death, and had gone to great trouble to provide refreshments for the reading (cookies that no one touched until Mark arrived and scarfed a few in a hungry, drunken fit).

When the rest of the writers finally straggled in, words were exchanged between several of the parties. Claire and Belinda had it out in American French. Mark apologized to Daisy for their lateness. Iona chided Daniel. It was an hour before things settled down, bruised egos patched up, wounds licked.

— — —

The swan song of the group became the reading of the story contest proposed at dinner in midweek, a story beginning with "That night at the café." As it turned out, only three were composed. Neil's was a humorously apocalyptic tale that began with "That night at the café, as the writers sat around waiting for the end of the world. . . ." Bess wrote an allegorical tale about a cat and horse, a twist on the *Animal Farm* paradigm. And Mark read his own encomium to the beauty and grace of Daisy and Iona, the mistresses of this Café du Coeur, placing his story in the misty past and describing them as possessing a famous charm that they inherited from their mother, whom he imagined an aristocrat:

— — —

Her full name was Anna Fernanda Carlotta Lourdes Domitia St. Germain Kristalszy, the Marquesa of You-Name-It-I've-Been-There. She was so beautiful the entire Austro-Hungarian army was in love with her, from the most highly decorated generals to the privates so low that to them gruel was like caviar. It was she who brought an end to the Hundred Years' War by threatening that, if both sides did not cease fighting, she would never leave her house again, but if she had to, she would cover her face in veils, wrap her body in sacs du potato, and wear ugly chapeaux made of corn husks and beehives.

His French was so painful that by this time in the trip he'd been nicknamed *Le Mangler*—the one who mangles any language he attempts. He seemed to have taken a British correspondence course in bad French, based on the castle scenes in Monty Python's *Search for the Holy Grail*, when he enunciated, in garbled Frenchified English, lines like, "I blow my nose in the hair of your mother, you tiny pig dog you." One could also detect the influence of the Warner Brothers' cartoon skunk Pepé Le Pew, who romances a sexy house cat with his French seduction technique, a faux-Charles Boyer parody that literally stinks up his animated, curly-cloud world. (When the cat wriggles out of his amorous embrace, he turns to the imagined audience and quips, "Perhaps she is playing hard to get, no?")

Needing a release from the tension and despair of the night's quarrels and the week's events, the group of writers laughed and applauded. After all three stories were read, the idea was voiced that there was no need for a winner or a loser, and the bottle of champagne was bestowed upon Daisy and Iona, for being the literary muses of all their efforts. By one in the morning the heavy wooden doors of the café had been locked, all the writers were in bed, the candles were blown out, the travel alarm clocks set to awaken them early enough to catch the buses and taxi rides to their trains and planes, to scurry back home to a sense of normalcy and routine.

And although it was virtually imperceptible, as they fell into the depths and deaths of their sleeps, the moon was already waning, having reached its peak earlier in the evening. The massive shape of our planet blue once again cast its shadow upon that white lunar sphere in the sky above, *la lune* now steering its course toward an ultimate waning, a dimming that would signify a time when its face would be forever shrouded in darkness, a time when, for each and every last one of them, this most ordinary cosmic entity would be invisible in the heady swoon of blackest night.

# Next Stop Palookaville

Gil Fieri, president and CEO of The Goal Line, Inc., a chain of athletic wear shops based in Dallas, was sitting in a field of black mud, cross-legged, in a circle three feet in diameter. He had drawn the circle in the mud himself, with a branch he'd found in the field. It was a spirit-father circle. As directed by the leader of the Wildman Gathering—who made a point of saying he'd been a "personal friend" of Robert Bly's—Gil had invited the image of his dead father into this circle. To confront him. To tell him off. To tell him all the things he never had the chance to tell him, since Gil's father had committed suicide forty-nine years ago, when Gil was three. He closed his eyes and tried to conjure up an image of his dead father in the circle, quickly rejecting the worm-filled eye sockets and hanging jawbone of the rotting, gruesome father that came to mind. Alas-poor-Yorick-I-knew-him-well. He struggled instead to visualize a young and healthy dad. But it wasn't easy. He never really knew what his father was like, and the only images he remembered were photographs.

He opened his eyes and stared into the circle. All he could see was the black mud of the field, peppered with white stones, and growing out of the mud, the dried brown stalks of dead sunflowers reaching over his head, crooked against the blue sky above. The cold of the wet field seeped through his khaki slacks, and all around him he heard screaming. Wild, guttural, stop-you're-torturing-me screams. We've had enough screams. A hundred yards to his right, another man in his own spirit-father circle was shouting, "Where were you when I needed you? You were never there! You bastard! I hate you!" Behind him, someone else screamed, "I needed you! Where were you, you son of a bitch! Get up off the ground! Look at me! What kind of coward are you? Look at me!" And beyond that, a lone, passionate voice screamed over and over again, "Help me! Help me! Help meeeee!"

Gil gave up on his father. With all this screaming, how's a person to think? His mind wandered. He'd gotten a speeding ticket on the drive there and for a moment flinched inwardly at the thought of paying it, and the insurance on his Jaguar going up again. But in a few days, that wouldn't matter anyway, would it? Still, we don't want to burn the bridges yet. Right now was a time for hoarding the eggs in the baskets, circling the wagons. Pulling in the horns, so to speak.

He thought about the infamous press release again, that started all this mess. So maybe he didn't have 24 stores in all. So maybe that wasn't exactly the truth. But what the heck, it's all just numbers, anyway, isn't it? Who's to say what's true and what isn't? Fraud's a big word, buddy. Don't go pointing a finger unless you want it broken off. Nancy Gillis. It's all *her* fault. Tell it to the D.A. So maybe it wasn't 24. Maybe it was 18. So sue me. What does that prove? Sales are *great* at those stores. That's not a lie. And so what if I'm a liar? Big deal. Sticks and stones may break my bones, but words will never hurt me.

Gil became aware of the cold damp on the seat of his pants. He checked his watch and realized it was time to return for more therapy. He had to concentrate and quit daydreaming. He had to focus. Focus pocus. He could still hear someone screaming. He stood up and brushed the dirt and sunflower stalks off his pants, thinking that he didn't remember them saying anything about *raving maniacs* in the brochure for this thing.

— — —

Gil Fieri was fifty-two years old and in better shape than most of his thirtysomething employees. He was six feet tall and weighed himself naked on his hospital-style cantilevered scales each morning at between 155 and 157 pounds. His hair was white and thin on top, his face ruddy and deeply lined. The skin of his neck had begun to show some slackness and wrinkling that bothered him, and he wondered if a little nip and tuck wouldn't be that much of a sin. *Who's it going to hurt? Who will be the wiser? I just think it's unprofessional to be sitting in a board meeting with a turkey wattle.* Gil ran five miles each evening after work at a consistent 8:15 pace, ate 2,000 calories of complex carbohydrates per day, and rarely drank alcohol.

He took a sometimes not-so-secret pride in his physical condition, as when he had the district managers check their resting pulse rate at a meeting and drew up a chart of it afterwards, with his name at the top, at an "athletic" 52, and Simon O'Donogue at the bottom, at 98. Two weeks later he called O'Donogue into his office and tossed him a printout of the chart, with a colored bar graph to show average pulse rates, the center being a neutral gray, his own rate of 52 at a cool Caribbean blue, and O'Donogue's high rate a fire engine red.

"I just wanted to show you this, and want you to take a good look at it."

O'Donogue blinked and put on a determined poker face as he regarded the chart, wondering how he was supposed to react. *Just tell me what you want, and I'll do it.* Simon believed himself to be quick on his feet, which he realized sometimes meant quick to bend over. He was a chunky man in his early forties who had risen from being a sales rep for Adidas to this district manager job at The Goal Line. He was married and had two children, a flair for numbers, and a weakness for pornography. He was sweating slightly inside his large-cut suit as he stared at the spectrum of colors on the sheet of paper in his hand, remembering those maps that always give you a falsely optimistic YOU ARE HERE, and thinking, this man is insane, but I guess if you're making eighty million a year gross you can afford to be crazy. Must be nice. Sit in here and call the slaves in for a little whipping. Well you'll get yours, pal. Just you wait. "Looks like I'm a little high here, doesn't it," he said.

Gil nodded. He leaned back in his chair and tapped the printout (he had his own from the color copier) with one finger. "You keep this up, Simon, and you won't be around here for long."

Simon blinked and shifted in his seat. As he tried to think of something to say, he realized his hands were sweating so much they were getting the printout damp. He laid it on the desk, the dark smudge marks of his hands clearly visible. He nodded nervously. He couldn't take Gil's direct stare and looked down at his damp, pudgy hands. When he spoke, his voice was faint and sounded what he thought would be properly contrite. "You mean I might wake up one morning and find myself unemployed?"

There was a pause as Gil stared at Simon and realized the misunderstanding. He shook his head. "No. Not at all. This isn't about your *job*, Simon. Hell, you're a good worker. I'm not talking about firing you. Forget that. I'm talking about your ticker." He tapped the left side of his chest. "Cardiac arrest. Blockage of arteries. Leading cause of death in white males between the ages of 35 and 60."

"Oh."

"Well that shouldn't make you feel any *better*. This isn't about a job. Who cares about a job? They're a dime a dozen. What I'm saying is you might wake up one morning and find yourself *dead.*"

— — —

Gil had been an All-American at S.M.U. in his senior year, and although he never had the speed of some of the other players, he had tenacity, a quality his coaches had called "heart," and that had carried him into the National Football League when salaries were still less than twenty thousand dollars a year. Even Gil's Italian last name had worked to his advantage then, since Vince Lombardi reigned as the coaching genius. Gil had been a mediocre cornerback for the Dallas Cowboys in the late 1960s, when Don Meredith was quarterback, and had retired early with a shoulder injury, getting a job at a Buick dealership, which eventually led him to owning two dealerships. But in the gas crunch of the mid-seventies he sold out and took advantage of the fledgling fitness craze by opening a sportswear shop.

He'd gotten a few endorsements from friends he still had in the NFL, local heroes mainly, a few appearances to open his stores in malls around the area. During the fall football season he'd done well with promotional endorsements, printing posters and calendars for the shops and having players like Lee Roy Jordan and Bob Lilly sign them. As shopping malls became popular Gil expanded to malls in Houston and San Antonio, so that by the 1980s he'd had eleven stores in Texas; at that point he began to dream big. He opened stores in California and North Carolina. He arranged with a securities dealer to take his company public at $19 a share, and it was a popular offering, coming into the end of the eighties bull market, shooting up to $31 a share within the first three weeks, then leveling off at $26. Within a few months Gil's personal assets had increased by almost nine million dollars. The Dallas *Morning News* did a story on the company, and the stock took off again.

That was when he hired Nancy Gillis as a public relations specialist. He gave her the project of infusing life and energy into the company's image. She suggested a "sexy" new television campaign featuring swimsuit models, volleyballs, and sunsets. She oversaw the development of a new corporate logo, and after being with the company only two months, was already close to Gil. One afternoon she arranged to be the last one to leave a late meeting in the conference room so she could walk to the elevator with Gil. She casually suggested that he join her and a female friend for drinks. Once she and Gil were installed comfortably at the bar, the fictitious friend quickly canceled via an equally fictitious telephone call placed by Nancy. That night they slept together. She was the first and only woman Gil had ever been intimate with who put a condom on him, so quickly he didn't realize what she was doing.

She arranged to get some good press for the company in small investor magazines, and even implied that *Business Week* and *Forbes* would be the next to follow. Then came the accident—really, she said, it was just an elaborate typo. She printed a press packet for him claiming there to be stores in Arkansas, Texas, Oklahoma, Missouri, Tennessee, California, Georgia, Alabama, Florida, North and South Carolina. Twenty-four stores in all. And no one ever proofed the press release, that is, no one outside the public relations department. Until finally Gil was reading a profile of his company in *Equities* magazine describing The Goal Line as an up-and-coming company, a bargain at $14 per share, quoting the misleading facts in the press release. He called Nancy at her office immediately, and she said, calm down, don't panic. And whatever you do, don't mention this to anyone. That night they met for drinks after work. Gil explained the errors in the article, but Nancy seemed nonplused.

"I don't have any stores in Oklahoma or Arkansas," he said.

"So?" she said, smiling. "Who can blame you? I wouldn't have any stores there either. I mean, those are only states in the loose sense of the word, aren't they?"

"This information is misleading."

"Really. Oklahoma. My God. Isn't that where they make all those nuclear bombs? A toxic wasteland of hillbilly mutants. Yuckola. No way. We are *not* opening a store there."

She tried to assuage Gil's fears of stockholder panic and fraud convictions, and by the third drink, Gil was aware of the persistent pressure of her leg against his under the table, and the danger of financial collapse seemed to wane as his erection waxed.

– – –

The beginning of the end—for Gil and his company—arrived via fax attack. One Thursday, analysts who followed the company at Dean Witter, Merrill Lynch, Shearson Lehman, and other professional traders began receiving faxes from an unidentified source alleging that The Goal Line was a fraud, that its accounting practices and inventory were falsified or unrealistic, that the number of stores it claimed to be in operation did not jibe with state tax records, and that the sales and earnings figures at the stores that were in existence were grossly inflated. They were. For the third quarter ending September 30, the published earnings per share figures were $1.62, up 23% from the e.p.s. of the previous year, while the fact of the matter was that they were probably lucky if the company had earned $1.20. Gil and the Chief Financial Officer had been able to conceal the figures by creative accounting—figuring in earnings to come in the next quarter and not counting payments to their creditors that should have already been made.

They had meant to return to accurate figures by waiting for their business to catch up to these inflated reports. They concealed the falsified books by hiring an unscrupulous accountant in Delaware who didn't question their figures. But the bear raid came too soon. Within two weeks the short position on the total shares outstanding had reached a disturbing 17%. At the first of October a San Francisco based publication called the Overpriced Stock Service published their research on the company, showing that there were no state tax records for the stores in Oklahoma and Arkansas, and that officials at the company would not give a straight answer when questioned over the telephone about it, other than the press release from Gil's office, "denying all allegations of wrongdoing." A mole planted inside the company's accounting department verified some suspicious information.

The weekend after the fax attack Gil turned off the ringer on his telephone, turned down the speaker volume on his answering machine, and sat on the couch, listlessly reading his tattered *Works of Shakespeare*. Before he remembered to disconnect his home fax, he received a note that said, WHAT WERE YOU THINKING?

Gil found himself lapsing into curious moments of absent-mindedness and whimsical reverie as his personal and professional life grew increasingly complicated, as the distinctions between truth and fiction faded from the black and white of certitude to an ashy and not particularly unattractive shade of gray, the color of cloudy skies before summer thunder. He found himself sitting at the desk of the Art Director of his in-house newsletter, staring at the electronic illustrations of fish and flying toasters of the screen saver software, while the Art Director, Lili Koenig, respectfully waited for him to get up from her chair and let her get back to work, and her assistant made a beats-me shrug behind his back, unable to explain his odd behavior. He found himself standing before a pyramid of oranges at the local health food supermarket and wondering what the odds of finding a perfectly round orange in the stack would be.

He felt weak and dizzy. His heart was beating too hard. He

couldn't keep any food down, and after a week of denying allegations, he'd lost five pounds. His palms kept sweating. Upon waking
up each morning, he dreaded getting out of bed. He dreaded getting
dressed, going to the office, facing his employees. He dreaded taking a shower. One of his old friends from his days at the Buick dealership, Louis Braude, told him about the Men's Movement, about
Robert Bly's book *Iron John*, and suggested that Gil go on a Wildman
Weekend to get in touch with his inner self.

— — —

As the others danced about the fire, randomly shouting and beating
the tom-toms, the Wildman facilitators, Coyote and Willow, urged
them on. The brassy flames leapt upward in the cold night air as if
heading toward the stars. Gil sat down on a rock and unlaced his
boots to remove a pebble that was killing him. A blister, too. The
absurdity of it, really, paying someone to tell you to loosen up and
howl at the moon. As if being alive weren't a good enough reason.
As the flames dwindled they quit dancing to thump on the drums
in unison, driving to a crescendo of noise, as if they were trying to
lure the Mighty Kong out of the depths of their being.

After these fractured fairy tales they noticed behind them, in
the sky, a patch of tangerine-colored light, like a rectangular cloud
filled with color and rays. "It's the Northern Lights!" cried someone. What do the lights signify? That before Caesar fell the graves
emptied out and the sheeted dead did speak and gibber in the Roman streets? Where do you hide from the reporters? How do you
clamp your hand over the mouth of a fax machine? The truth?

— — —

The next day, after they supervised the screaming at absentee fathers in the spirit-father circles, Willow and Coyote divided the
men into groups. These were demarcated depending on the nature of their dysfunction. Domineering mothers, hostile-abusive

fathers, nice-but-too-busy pops, and sarcastic dads seemed to hover over the clusters of middle-aged men in a field. Gil was included with the absent-father group. There were five of these men. Gil was the last to speak. He listened as the others tearfully related how their fathers were never around the house, and how they always missed them. They leaned against the oak trees and wiped tears from their eyes as they told about the fishing trips they never went on, the Christmases without pop. Gil told how his father had committed suicide when he was three years old, how his older brother had also done so before the age of thirty-five.

"I don't know why they did it," he said. "I don't know. I was too young when my father did it, and I could never really talk to my brother. But I'm the only male left in my family. Sometimes I feel like I'm the next to go. But I don't want to."

The men hugged and told him not to do it. It would be such a waste. Gil nodded guiltily and wiped the half-tears from his eyes. What a dirty sneak. If they only knew. Here they are spilling their guts, and look at me. A spy in their midst. A sneak-thief.

— — —

Next they all formed a giant circle and were urged to testify. After several tales of woe and abuse, Gil raised his hand. "Yes, brother. Tell us what's on your mind," said Coyote.

He stood and brushed off the seat of his pants. "Hi. My name is Gil and I'm the head of a corporation. But I'm an impostor. Everyone thinks of me as a great decision-maker and a shrewd businessman, but it's not true. I really don't know what I'm doing. Any day now my life is going to fall apart completely. I've only gotten as far as I have through luck, and I think that's about to run out. I really don't make any decisions or shrewd deals, I just go with the flow and take advantage of some opportunities. The only reason I got into business in the first place was through some connections on my football team. And they just wanted a former NFL player. And even when I played, I was always just faking it. I never really cared whether we won or not. I always preferred reading to sports, but people seemed to like me more when I played sports. And I seemed to be good at it. Although it was all just luck."

Toward the end of his testimonial Gil's voice had begun to shake and he felt like crying, but he wouldn't let himself. Shouts and choruses of "Ho!" filled the air as he was speaking, and someone patted his back at the end, while Coyote said, "I know exactly how you feel. You think you're an impostor. You feel like you're fooling everyone. That they don't know the truth, the real you."

"Ho!"

"Me too! That's exactly how I feel!"

"But you've got to realize that you're wrong. That you're smart and talented, or you wouldn't be where you are today. That being the president of a corporation isn't easy, and you didn't make it there through dumb luck."

"But you don't see," said Gil. "You don't understand." He looked at Coyote, then around at his fellow wildmen in the circle. "I *am* an impostor. I'm a liar. I'm not really who I say I am, or what I say I am. I'm a fake. A cheat."

Coyote told the group that this was typical of the Impostor Phenomenon, this denial of the truth of one's accomplishments. "The victim of the Impostor Phenomenon doesn't *feel* like a fake, to himself, he *is* a fake." As an antidote to this, Coyote told them, "You need to tap your warrior well. That immense vat of emotions inside you. That volcano inside you that is a source of strength, of grieving."

Gil decided to keep his mouth shut. He'd almost blown everything. One more word and his alibi would have been dead meat. Coyote went on to say that almost 70% of successful people suffer from some symptoms of the Impostor Phenomenon. And what occurred to Gil was that maybe those 70% were right. Maybe they *were* impostors. Like himself. And like this charlatan of a pop psychologist, a pseudo-Sigmund, working with two parts pep talk and one part Indian mumbo-jumbo.

— — —

After leaving the Wildman Gathering on the ranch near Waco, Gil drove the two hundred miles to Mustang Island, stopping at convenience stores along the way for Styrofoam cups of coffee, waxing nostalgic already at what he'd be leaving behind. His mouth felt like a volcano. I give you this, all this, and so much more. It's that undiscovered country jazz. That dread of something after death. Puzzles the will. At the intracoastal canal he drove onto the ferry, a worker in orange reflective jacket waving him into the parking space, using his arms in semaphore, the seafood air soft into the night around him. He turned the wipers on to clear the spray from his windshield, but they only smeared it into two arcs.

Once on the island, he followed the access road for ten miles before turning off the pavement into the deep sand, keeping to the ruts in the road, having to gun his engine to keep from getting stuck. His headlights illuminated only a few feet of sand in front of him, and he drove slowly, swerving to avoid driftwood and beach debris. He rolled his window down. The surf sounded amplified, and the wind filled his ears and buffeted his thin hair. After a mile or so, when he had passed no cars, he turned the wheels in toward the water, pulled onto the deep soft sand at the waves' wet edge, and killed the engine.

The sea seemed quieter, with the car blocking out the wind. He sat and felt his heart racing. His eyes adjusted to the darkness. Soon he could see the frothy white caps of the sloppy waves breaking and rushing toward him. He saw sea birds—gulls or terns probably—skimming over the shore. The sky above was black and covered with clouds. He got out of the car and sat in the sand, looking up at the tented dark, stars only visible through gaps in the clouds.

My hour's almost come. When I to sulfurous and tormenting flames must render up myself. But it's that conscience that makes cowards of us all. When the native hue of resolution is sicklied over with the pale cast of thought. He unlaced his expensive wingtips and hurled them toward the breakers. He unrolled his socks, feeling the cold night damp of the sand, struck with the image of ashtrays. He unbuttoned the rest of his clothing and tossed it down onto the sand, until he was completely naked. He shivered, hugged himself as he stepped to the car and popped the latch on the trunk.

From the trunk he took a paper sack of old clothes and put them on. Luckily there was still no one driving down the beach. He pulled on the baggy pair of blue jeans, sweater, and floppy hunting jacket, then put a night watchman's sailor cap on his head. I look like a killer on *Mannix* or *Baretta*, he thought, his heart still racing. He still shivered violently, although he was suddenly suffused with the warmth of the old clothes. This cold night will turn us all to fools and madmen. Poor Tom's a cold. Croak not, black angel, I have no food for thee. And pulling the rucksack from the trunk, he ran across the ruts of the beach road into the dunes. He knew how far he had to walk, how to follow the beach access road for eleven miles to Flour Bluff, where a Greyhound station waited, and a bus south, to the border.

By eleven o'clock that morning the San Patricio County Sheriff's Deputy Davis Deeks had gotten his uniform wet up to his knees wading into the surf, collecting the evidence of the "floater." The car had been searched and three hundred and fifty-eight dollars had been found in Gil's wallet. A missing person's report would be filed, but they were going to wait for forty-eight hours, according to federal regulations.

By two o'clock Gil had walked across the international bridge over the Rio Grande between Matamoros and Brownsville. He was headed for the Caribbean. There was $7,000 in his rucksack and money belt, a tight roll of twenties in his shoes. Another $892,000 in a safe deposit box in Port Au Prince. And in Switzerland, still more. He had done his research. There would be no passport check until the *aduana* at 15 miles into the country, and none at all for the bus he was taking. Besides, his passport was an expensive fake. His name was now David Conroy. He liked the sound of it. As he waited for the bus south to Vera Cruz, he peeled an orange. He enjoyed the tang of it. He couldn't remember the last time he'd dug his thumb into the skin, getting the white membrane under his fingernails. Years, probably. The simple pleasures.

— — —

At five o'clock, the bus pulled into the oil-spattered lane of the station to depart. He boarded as a cloud of diesel smoke chugged out of its rusted muffler. A short, fat Mexican woman pushed in front of him, carrying two huge burlap baskets, one filled with white onions, the other with bright red tomatoes. Gil realized he was going to have to make some changes. *La boleta, por favor. Gracias.* He sat in the front seat so he could keep an eye on the driver. You never know about these people. The naugahyde upholstery of the old school bus was ripped and patched with duct tape.

For a moment, Gil struggled with the slats of the windows, hearing the ratcheting clacking of them being lowered by the other passengers in the back of the bus as it filled up, but his wouldn't budge. He sat down and took a paperback out of his pack. Yes, some changes were in order. I'm a common man now, no more king of the jungle. With his book open in his lap, he stared out the window at the driver, a balding man with a wrinkled forehead, about his age, and watched as he talked to the baggage handler loading suitcases into the bus.

The driver was smoking a cigarette before boarding for departure, and Gil watched this, thinking, You better lay off the coffin nails, pal. But it's your grave. Me, I'll be fine. Long as this bus doesn't have lice. Louse? Or maybe flea. Flee. Yes. Of course. No. I'll be fine. As long as I don't drink the water. Fleas. Flees. The cat will mew, and the dog will have his day.

# The Hidden Jesus

The electrician did not want to speak. He stared at the ceiling and scratched his muscled forearm, on which was tattooed the name Sarah, with a circle/bar over it. He was here to avoid jail time and that was it. He preferred to keep his yap shut.

That wasn't good enough. That wasn't part of the plan. He had to speak. They made him do it. They said, Tell us about your life. Tell us how it feels. Shegog, the Pain & Suffering Workshop leader, said they could wait. We can wait as long as it takes, he added. Redemption is in no hurry.

In this box of silence, Sanchez stared at his shiny black wingtips, new and loose, like the borrowed shoes of a dead cop. He heard coughs. A defrocked priest with a sweet potato nose and eyes like pools of sadness slowly ripped a white paper napkin into smaller and smaller pieces. Hull, the security guard, watched him do this. He wanted to grab the priest's hands and make him stop, but he didn't. The Pain & Suffering Workshop was all about learning to do what did not come naturally. Hull imagined the napkin shreds projected into smaller and smaller divisions, like a reflection of mirrors facing mirrors, seeing yourself in ever-shrinking reflections down to the size of an eyelash morphing to a tiny peacock tail.

When the electrician cracked (as they all did eventually, it was only a matter of time), his chin trembled. All looked away. It was ugly business, this giving in. The electrician said his name was Sanchez and that he was an alcoholic, a drug addict, a sexaholic. Crystal meth, adultery, insurance fraud. You name it, he said. I done it. I'm a louse. I once stole from a March of Dimes box, for Chrissakes.

Shegog closed his eyes and nodded. Go on, he said. You are on the path to light.

Sanchez sighed and rubbed his watery eyes. I did some bad things. I threatened my wife with an extension cord because she refused to do me anymore. So I shouted at her. I said, You don't want me to touch you anymore, how about this? So I looked around and the first thing I could find was an extension cord and I yanked it out the wall and dragged her by her arm and tried to whip her with it.

He paused and shook his head. He went on: She grabbed the refrigerator door and squirmed away, and I started to feel bad. I just couldn't do it. The look on her face, Jesus. I kept pulling on her and finally she let go and I dropped the extension cord. I twisted her wrist a little, but I really didn't hurt her bad. Still she never forgave me for that. No sirree. You bet I heard about that, and will hear about it the rest of my goddamn fucking life. Welcome to Disneyland.

The others in the room stared at their feet. They sat in a conference room in a Christian rehabilitation center. Out the window, in the distance, loomed a snow-capped peak. Everyone called it Sorry Mountain.

Get it out, said the defrocked priest.

Jewel, the travel agent with the rough voice of a screamer, scowled. Oh, right, she said. Thanks for sharing. If you ask me, this creep ought to be shot, is what he ought to be.

Shegog frowned. Nobody is shooting anyone. That isn't helpful.

No, you're right, said Jewel. Not shot. I'm sorry. That's too good for him, she hissed. Maybe ground up slowly on a meat grinder. Like, one hand at a time.

Now now, said Shegog. As head counselor, he'd already admitted he had once been a drunk and a heel himself. We're in the comfort zone right now, aren't we? This is where we share. This is where we listen.

Fine and dandy, said Jewel. I listen. I heard. I just happen to think shit for brains here, Sanchez, doesn't deserve to live. That's just my opinion, right? It's a free country. Last time I checked.

We all deserve to live, said the priest.

Ha ha. Very funny.

Let her speak, said Sanchez. I can take it. No rules, no boundaries, right? And that means no secrets. If she thinks it but doesn't say it, then it's a secret. I know all about secrets, he said. Believe me. I used to screw my sister-in-law whenever she came to babysit Esteban. Karen would be away working the night shift and I'd do Sheila in my in-laws' RV parked in the driveway. We'd pull the curtains shut and fuck like there was no tomorrow. I can sit here and feel guilty about it all I want, sure, but tell the truth? I loved it. It was different and, man, I needed that.

If being bad didn't have its special moments, we'd all be good, right? He grinned. First we'd put Esteban to bed and if he was too wound up we'd fill his bottle with beer. After he passed out we'd go at it. Sheila liked me to hold her wrists down tight like I was a cat burglar or something and I'd just caught her by surprise, my pockets full of fucking pearl necklaces. Now? Well, go figure. I'm divorced and don't even have visitation rights to see my son. Sheila and Karen? They still talk. They've gotten over it. Me? I'm the bad guy. So that's my story.

You people are disgusting, said Jewel. I should have booked a trip to Mazatlán and got shit-faced on margaritas.

— — —

Outside the sun burned upbeat and optimistic. Beyond the claustrophobic interrogation rooms of the rehab center sparkled snow-dusted peaks of the Rocky Mountains like pop-up ads for scenic beauty. From the back of the recreation center a path led to an abandoned ski resort. The air there smelled forgotten and innocent. With the climate change of the last few years there had been a snow drought, and not enough fell to keep the ski resort in powder. The slopes were grassy and wide. The ski lift T-bars swung gently in the wind.

The Christian management who now ran the abandoned ski resort often referred to the former skiers as sinners and profligates who enjoyed the self-indulgent pastime of sliding downhill on wooden planks only second to sodomy or child molesting, and preferred, if they could get it, all in the same alcohol-fueled weekend sprees.

During the afternoon break Sanchez killed time, trimming his toenails. The conference center was adorned with crucifixes and lilies, which made Sanchez feel guilty just thinking the thoughts in his head, the thoughts that came naturally and without his bidding. His brain seemed a satellite television system over which he had no control, no remote, no nothing.

He lay in his rehab dorm room beneath a small painting of the infinitely gentle, master-of-suffering Jesus H. Christ, and remembered the hot tidal surge of want that swept him toward his sister-in-law. She had a sense of vulnerability and readiness, an aura of Do Me Now. Like, if he caught her in the basement, as he did, as he had more than once, folding clothes on the wooden table beside the dryer. If he caught her there and came up behind her and kissed her neck softly and with feeling, no matter how important it was that Christ died for our sins, she would whimper and squirm and never would she resist.

She would simply lean over the wooden table and knock the box of laundry detergent to the floor. Tide it was, and tied she would be, her wrists bound with a terrycloth belt pulled from a robe clean and fresh from the dryer. He would lift her skirt and she would never say no. She would only say Hurry. Hurry, she would say: Someone might come down, she would whisper. I don't want them to see us like this.

Why not? he wanted to ask. Why can't they see us as we are? Not as we pretend to be? Because we are base. Because we are damned. Because we are not. Not what? What we pretend to be. We are lesser beings in our unguarded moments. Only a veneer of responsibility and respectability keeps us from degradation and disappointment, an image of the true hunger and seething that unfolds in constant heartbeat time in all of us.

Beneath the idealized and infinitely gentle portrait of Jesus he imagines his sister-in-law bent upon the table as if suffering him to enter her were a form of prayer. Sanchez remembered kneeling in the pews of St. Matthews cathedral, where he had taken communion, mouth open, tongue awaiting the body of Christ, where he had said his prayers of penitence for years before discarding this life of a Hebrew folk hero as so much well-intentioned hooey.

She, his succubus, his fallen angel, *la hermana política*, clutched the sides of the wooden table and whispered but not in pain or retribution or condemnation. She whispered in secret thrill and conspiracy for him to do what he wanted, what she wanted, what a man should want, what a woman should want. What both should never admit or give in to but they did.

They could not help themselves.

He finished with a shudder and, panting still, his head dizzy with the gush and heat of feeling, he zipped his pants and composed himself beneath the portrait of Christ. An ideal he could never reach, a life he could not, would not want to ape or emulate. He had no patterns to fit, no molds into which to squeeze his forms. He had only sins to want and after tasting to be punished for. Still the portrait of Christ hung above him and would to the end of his days and suffer he would in its shadow of piety.

— — —

Hull the security guard walked with Jewel the travel agent through an old West cemetery at the foot of Sorry Mountain, in the golden fields of a forgotten prairie, past tumbleweeds clumped against the barbed-wire fence. He did his best to separate himself from the other buffaloes in the rehab ranch herd.

I mean, sure, I did some bad things. I was a cop for a while, and sure, not all of my evidence reached the courtroom, you know what I'm saying? I might have snagged some party supplies here and there, sure. But Jesus, I never did my sister-in-law.

Score one for you, said Jewel.

I've never even hit a woman. If I saw someone hit a woman, I swear, I'd kill him.

Okay, now. Don't get carried away.

They stopped before a bleached wood tombstone: CYRUS HAND, 1863–1888.

Jewel nodded. A man of few words. I bet he slapped around a few saloon gals.

He's dead now, said Hull.

Your turn is next, said Jewel.

To die?

To speak.

Oh. That's good. Or not.

Now we get to hear.
Hear what?
What it is. You know. Your secret.
Hull shrugged. The usual.
I doubt that.

— — —

Seated at the center of the circle of sharing, Shegog looked shabby
biblical, a discount liquor store prophet. His legs were painfully
thin, and crossed awkwardly, as feeble as the arms of an old man
embittered with failure and recrimination. His beard wizened and
scraggly, his eyes blue-shadowed and droopy, both testified to the
harsh life of a boozehound. Sharing the same room with him was
like visiting a dead relative momentarily retrieved by the mumbo
jumbo of a medium, one who had not expected company, his living
room in the afterlife musty and cluttered. The jagged furrows in his
grayish, gaunt face repulsed and fascinated Jewel, who wondered if
the man had ever been foolish in love.

Following the line of his gaze up her skirt and between her legs,
she squeezed her thighs tighter, then draped her sweater over them,
like a drop cloth over a work of art. Pulling at his Egyptian desert
beard, Shegog looked saddened and defeated toward the now hidden gems of Jewel.

The world is not done, he said. Ask yourself, do people change?
Does anything ever change? Does it seem that we are doomed to
repeat our errors? I shall give you an answer. The world is not done.
The world is not over. Every moment of motion is a moment of
change. Yes, the patterns are established. The patterns are in place.
They are not fixed. We step outside the boundaries. We create new
ones. There is room for redemption as well as for sin and chaos.
Speak not only with your tongues but with your bones and fingers.
Sanchez here shamed himself by pulling down the pants of his

sister-in-law and thrusting himself inside her, his weak and gasping child mewling and hungry in the corner.

Shegog continued, his voice a beaten, swayback horse of god: Angry at his wife for scolding his sorrowful drunkenness, Sanchez berated his wife's father for raising such a worthless woman and shouted he'd see them all in Hell before he spent another night in that house.

Shegog's voice then dropped into a coarser and deeper growl. Before leaving he violated his hapless sister-in-law on the pool table of his game room.

Now wait a minute, said Sanchez. It was not actually on the pool table. Give me some credit. We were on the couch, for Chrissakes.

— — —

What the other rehab people did not know:

His sister-in-law was not a beautiful or funny or intelligent or glamorous woman. What made her remarkable was that she would feel for you, she could feel for a person. If you had a bad day and she asked you How is everything? and you told her, as Sanchez had, many times, My life sucks, she wouldn't just ignore it. She wouldn't tell you to get over it. She would ask Why? She would want you to tell her about it. She wouldn't laugh at you and tell you how pathetic you were, that you'd been going downhill for a long time but now you'd reached bottom, or if not bottom you were close to it.

She would never say that.

Instead she would hold you in her arms as if you were a child, as if you were a baby, and in her arms you would weep and in that weeping you would be cleansed. The first time she had held Sanchez in her arms he had been surprised. He'd told her how he'd been late to work and how it wasn't his fault, how the traffic had been backed up on the freeway, this head-on collision with people killed and everything, the jaws of life prying car doors open to remove the bloody, mangled bodies of a woman and her daughter. But his boss didn't buy it. He said, Sanchez? You know what you're problem is?

Sanchez hated that. When your boss asked if you knew what your problem was? It was never good news. It never meant you were getting a raise or a day off or a bonus. It meant you were getting fucked, is what it meant. So when his boss asked him that, he said *nada*. He just stared. His face didn't move: *Point a gun at me. Between my eyes. I will not flinch.*

The problem with you, Sanchez, is that you're what I'd call a sorry person. You're always telling me how sorry you are. I'm sorry for this and I'm sorry for that. While, personally, I don't give a shit. After a while I don't hear it. You're just sorry. I look at you and I think, That's one sorry son of a bitch. Sanchez's boss then shook his head and turned away. Get the fuck outta here, he said. Take your sorry ass somewhere else. Somewhere I don't have to look at you.

When Sanchez told his sister-in-law this, she said, Oh, that's not true. The next thing she held him close. Her body was warm and soft. Into her he melted. Through her he burned.

Don't hide from the light, said Shegog. His hoarse voice sounded like Moses through the PA system of a hamburger hut. Shine the light on the darkness of your soul and it shall be bleached.

Yeah, well. I'm all for light and darkness, but—

Shegog held up his hand for Sanchez to be silent. He sighed. He spoke directly to the soul of each person seated in the circle. We must reach the bottom before we can look up. Above is redemption and the resurrection. For the penitent, there is money and forgiveness.

All right then, said Sanchez. Amen. Ain't nothing else to do but admit the truth and move on. Life ain't over yet.

Did he say *money* and forgiveness? asked Jewel. She leaned toward Hull, whispering. Did I hear right?

Which brings us to Mr. Hull. I believe it's your turn to speak. Tell us why you're here.

Hull sighed and cracked his knuckles. He looked at the carpeted floor in front of him, scorched black here and there by fallen cigarettes, as if he were about to read his sins from a floor-mounted teleprompter. Well my name is Hull and I guess you would say I'm an alcoholic. I never thought of myself that way but you know to tell the truth I never thought too much one way or the other. Nobody's perfect, right? But because of all my DUIs and all I lost my job and now they tell me if I do some time here in rehab I won't lose my license which is why I'm here so here I am. He shrugged. I mean, I'm not Charlie Manson if that's what you're thinking. Then again I'm no boy scout.

You lost your job, said Shegog. You were an officer of the law and you brought shame upon your brothers in uniform.

I guess. Two sides to every story, though. I didn't do half of what they say I did.

You pulled over a teenage girl for speeding and had sex with her in your patrol car in exchange for ripping up the ticket.

Hull folded his arms across his chest. He wouldn't look up. That's her story, he said.

Shegog stroked his wiry beard. His heavy eyelids closed and he continued without the need for sight. You fathered an illegitimate child in the back seat of your patrol car, while her wrists were handcuffed.

That was her idea, not mine. In the hearing the lawyer called her consenting but truth is it was she who lassoed me. I was just dumb enough to fall for it is what the truth is. That girl had an imagination and then some.

Shegog softened. So none of this is your fault? Is that what you claim?

I claim nothing. I did wrong. I know that. Hull lifted his chin and looked at the others: Shegog, Sanchez, Jewel, Father X. You know what started it all? I lied about my age. That's what I think started it all. When I was thirty-two I decided to tell everyone I was twenty-seven. This was after my first wife died and I met all new people. No one from my old life was around. So I changed some details.

You didn't like who you had become.

Do you? asked Hull. Do you like yourself?

You don't have to like, said Jewel. Maybe just accept.

Who gives a shit? asked Sanchez. After all is said and done, isn't it just all blah blah fucking blah?

Shegog uncrossed his wino legs and fished a Camel from his front pocket. What say we take five. Look at the time. Lunch snuck up on us like beer goggles, didn't it? I understand today there is fried chicken and cole slaw. He grinned. Like mama used to make.

Hot damn, said Sanchez.

My sentiments exactly, said Shegog. We'll get back to this later and take another stab at the throat of our nature.

— — —

Hull followed Jewel to the cemetery at the bottom of the hill, carrying their lunch in a brown paper bag spotted dark with oil from the fried chicken. They headed toward the cemetery for the comfort of ghosts. For the understated wisdom of epitaphs. Both Hull and Jewel disliked people, especially when they gathered around you, fallen and fly-buzzed, as they gossiped and croaked, as they picked at your bones.

The smell of the chicken seeped from the bag and followed them through the pines and aspens like an invisible dog. It reminded Hull of his childhood and how all those years ago he had been poor and happy and surrounded by his mother and eight brothers and sisters. Now his mother and two of his siblings were dead and the rest of them so far away and out of touch they might as well be. He realized three of his sisters he would probably never see alive again. What was the point? Surrounded by these stones, by these gray tombstones on a windy prairie hill, he knew it was foolish to expect ultimate meaning. This gut feeling of pointlessness may be honest but didn't make it any easier.

Sitting on the log bench beside Jewel, Hull was chilled by the fall wind. He watched the yellow aspen leaves clatter against the tombstones. Hull lifted his head and tried to give Jewel a smile. He had reached a point in his life when a melancholy nostalgia was as constant as the graying hairs in his scalp. It now seemed that all his life—all memories and visions of his past, his successes and failures, his loves and heartbreaks—were at the tip of his tongue. And this accumulation of past weighed on him like a reversed iceberg, with his visible self just the white and icy tip, and the dark submerged aqua weight of his past suspended above him in a cloud as big as the Atlantic.

Jewel was speaking and he had not heard.

Earth to Hull, come in, Hull.

I'm sorry, he said. I'm here. He shook his head. I'm drifting.

I know the feeling, said Jewel.

— — —

As part of the cleansing process at Sorry Mountain, the penitents were required to drink a great amount of water. Ten eight-ounce glasses a day, minimum. The Water Treatment it was called, and second in importance only to confession and submission to the will of a moody God. Their bladders swelled and they left the Circle of Sharing frequently to relieve themselves, the path of purity smelling distinctly of urine.

Like Hull, Jewel acknowledged the only reason her train stopped at Sorry Mountain was to avoid jail time. Plus to clean up her act.

I'm no different than anyone else, she said. I've done some things I'm not proud of. I'm no angel.

That's where you're wrong, said Shegog. He insisted there was an angel inside of Jewel, waiting to be released. Think of it as The Hidden Jesus. There is a Jesus hidden inside all of us. Merciful and just, forgiving and kind. A man we would like to be, a man glowing with love and glory.

I've had many men inside of me, said Jewel. Some of them glowed, too. But I didn't want to be any of them.

Sanchez laughed, the defrocked priest grinned. Only Shegog scowled. The men you have touched called to you in voices of despair and self-loathing, the ventriloquists of lust.

And I returned the call, said Jewel. I star sixty-nined it. Her voice was faint and penitent. She told how she had seduced her psychology professor in his office, years before, in her graduate studies at college.

We did it on his desk, she said. I wore this blue jean skirt. I could tell he liked it. Then he started acting funny and said something about how he needed to save his marriage. He dumped me for his wife. She looked up at the group and smiled bitterly. So I got him back. I told the administration what we'd done, how he'd said it would help my grade. He never said that. I added that. I thought of it as extra credit. He had all these rules about how you could get extra credit in his class. So I made up my own, and claimed it came from him.

I got him fired and shamed and I was glad of it, too. He had me, so I had him. After he was finished, I felt good. I really did. We were even. Now, I don't know.

The ex-priest coughed. He'd already told about having sex with altar boys, so he wasn't about to point the finger.

Well now, said Sanchez. We're not exactly little Miss Perfect, are we? And you thought I was disgusting.

You are, said Jewel.

Oh, right. All I know is I didn't ruin anyone's life.

What about that sister-in-law? hissed Jewel.

Sanchez shrugged. She doing just fine.

— — —

In the cemetery, Hull and Jewel poked among the golden prairie grass and the tombstones gray and iconic. They stood before a small stone cross. Inscribed in worn and faded letters was the legend: DALVA HASSELBECK, August 4, 1881-September 21, 1883. BLESS THIS LAMB, NOW IN THE LORD'S LOVING ARMS.

Jewel had been crying. Her nose was pink and her long eyelashes matted. I was never the lamb of the Lord, she said. I've been a bad girl since I can remember. I mean, I used to imagine what it would be like to have sex with the Tooth Fairy.

I've lied about my age all my life, said Hull. That part about changing my age being the turning point in my life? That's bullshit. For one thing, my name isn't Hull. I never liked my real name so after high school I came up with something better.

What's your real name?

Leonard.

I don't blame you. But still. I don't get it.

Get what?

Why are you here? You changed your name. You lied about your age. You lost your job. Big deal. You don't belong here. I'm a bigger fake than you are. You want to know the truth? Even my breasts aren't real, said Jewel. She rubbed tears from her face. They're as fake as the rest of me.

I have my reasons, said Hull. You don't know—

You're a fake too, is what I think. You just came here to soak up some pity. That's what I think.

Jewel waited for a reply. She watched a red-tailed hawk kite and soar over the prairie. She read the name on tombstones bedecked with American flags and plastic flowers. ANNA, WIFE OF J.T. SKIN-

NER. BORN JUNE 20, 1831. DIED SEPTEMBER 9, 1881. MOTHER IS NOT DEAD BUT SLEEPETH/WE WILL MEET AGAIN.

When she turned to look for Hull, he was on the other side of the cemetery, his inscrutable face glowing with a halo of golden sunset light.

— — —

The trouble with Hull was that he didn't believe in redemption.

He didn't believe he would ever truly change or that life would ever be essentially different. He walked between the rows of tombstones and took great care not to tread upon the graves. The names were of English or German ancestry, and he reasoned that for many of those people, those lives, this was their only record. JOHN SUTHERLAND, 1848–1883. Faded epitaph on a limestone tablet. ELIZA HAMILTON, 1888. Died 3 months, 16 days. BLESSED CHILD, LIE DOWN MY LAMB, TAKE UNTO THEE THIS SLEEP.

Is that all? What record will I leave? he wondered. A life of bitterness and resentment, a life of compulsive longing and surrender to the rut? What virtues will they remember me for? My family? My wife? Years after my death and disappearance from this world, will I be mentioned or honored? He paused before a guitar-shaped monument, at the foot of which lay a garland of plastic flowers, and he realized the gaping mouth of emptiness and unimportance opening wide its chapped lips to swallow him.

— — —

In the Pain & Suffering Workshop, Shegog announced that today perhaps it would be best to refocus their efforts on absolution. Sanchez had admitted to his depravity and Jewel had detailed her life as a vengeful temptress. The sins of all the others, including the apostasy of the defrocked priest, had been lanced like a suppurating wound and exposed to the curative oxygen of public scrutiny.

We must not have any private behavior, said Shegog. If all that we do and think is known, we will be cleansed.

Only one man remains who has not been set free, said Shegog. As his hoarse voice weakened to a whisper, all were silent and squeamish. Only one man, he added, has refused to see the light of our Lord Jesus Christ.

Hull cringed as if he were the honoree of a celebrity roast. His task to grin and bear it. We were having an argument about one of my old girlfriends, he said. It all seems so stupid now. For some reason, Dianne was jealous of her. This was a few years ago, with Dianne, my first wife. We were drinking too much back then and it seems everything would be fine one moment and the next, I'd say something wrong and she'd say something wrong and it would set us off and we'd be at each other's throats. For hours. So we were on this camping trip in the mountains, kind of trying to dry out, I guess. Clean out our pipes. Breathe some fresh air.

I said Let's hike up to the waterfalls and have a picnic lunch. It was a beautiful day and everything was going great. The sky was so blue it hurt to look up. Plus we saw moose. Dianne was so excited. She had never seen a moose.

I don't know why it turned out so badly. It just did. I'm sure it's all my fault at some Freudian, subconscious level, but, really, I didn't mean to hurt Dianne. It was an accident.

There are those who believe there are no accidents, said Shegog. That what we do and what happens to us occurs for a reason. The will of God.

That's bullshit, said Sanchez. The other night I hit a deer when I was driving home from work. And I don't care what you say. It was an accident. Plain and simple.

We are always under the watchful gaze of the Lord, said Shegog.

Right, said Sanchez. The way of the Lord are mysterious, blah blah blah frickin' blah.

Let the man tell his story, said Jewel.

I don't know what got us started on it, but somehow I told Dianne I thought she needed to wear a skirt now and then. A nice dress, I said. You'd look good in it. She always wore jeans and I told her I didn't like her looking like a goddamn teenage boy all the time.

That set her off. She said I was sick and perverted. That my wanting her to wear a skirt was just another way to say I wanted to use her. She said it proved what a warped individual I was. She said, Why I ever married you, I don't really know.

Well, go, then. Get out of here, I shouted. You're not such a fucking catch yourself, you know that? You know that? Miss High and Mighty.

She stormed off, down the trail beside the waterfall. It was steep and slippery. And at first I just watched her. Then she disappeared into the gully beside the waterfall, in the rainbow haze of its spray, and I couldn't see her anymore. I started down in a hurry to catch up with her. I rushed across the scree and after a few steps the whole slope started to slide and hiss with falling rocks. They clattered off the cliffs below me, above Dianne, and sent an avalanche of rock into the gully.

The first thing I saw, before I found her, was blood on the cliffs. A big rock cut a gash in her head and when I reached her, she was sitting at the edge of the waterfall, blood streaming down her face and neck. Dianne was wincing and rubbing the sticky wound at the top of her head. I'm not giving it back, she said. It's mine and you can't have it. She turned away and began to stumble down the steep trail.

Wait. Let me look at you, I told her.

You can't have it back, she said, not turning around. Blood streaked down her arm, mixing wet with the spray from the waterfall.

Have what back?

My engagement ring. You gave it to me and it's mine. What kind of cheap bastard wants his engagement ring back? Just because you don't love me anymore doesn't give you a right to take your gifts back.

Then she was screaming at me. Screaming all these things she must have been thinking for a long time, but she had never said before. Over and over again she screamed, YOU HAVE ALWAYS BEEN A CHEAP BASTARD! Then she got quiet.

I grabbed her arm and she jerked it away. But she did turn and look at me. I had never seen such a look on her face. It was revulsion. It was hatred. She sneezed then, spraying a fine splatter of blood droplets upon the gray stones of the cliff.

I don't feel so good, she said. She sat down in the trail. Then she grimaced and slumped over and died right in my arms.

Hull was silent. He lifted his face to the others, who had nothing to say. Jewel wept. He turned to Shegog and said, So there you go. Does that make me any cleaner?

Shegog droned something about redemption and forgiveness. Hull paid no attention. He walked out onto the deck to stare at Sorry Mountain and smoke a cigarette. His hands were shaking. He placed them on the deck railing to steady them.

— — —

That night the air turned cold and still. They woke to a darkened sunlight as at dusk and the mountains cloaked in a shroud of clouds. Snow fell throughout the day and settled a pall of blue shadows in the rooms of the rehab center. There was a lull in the meetings and all were asked to read inspirational literature and drink as much water as their bodies could possibly stand. The defrocked priest had to be urged and cajoled to get out of bed and when he did so his eyes were bloodshot and remorseful, his steps hesitant and pained. He and Sanchez shared a cabin.

Shegog asked Sanchez to keep an eye on the priest, to try to be encouraging, to find the good man in his heart and urge him to come forward. Sanchez nodded and kept his eyes upon the page of *Chicken Soup for the Recovering Soul*. As soon as Shegog left the cabin Sanchez placed the book upon his chest and closed his eyes. He was waiting for the afternoon. He had plans. With his eyes closed he listened to the defrocked priest complain of headaches and being unable to breathe, how he could never seem to catch his breath. I don't think I'm long for this world, he said.

Don't be so dramatic, said Sanchez, looking into the blackness of his eyelids. It's the altitude.

The priest began to whisper a litany of prayer and to this mumbled devotion Sanchez fell to sleep. He woke after a while and looked across the room to the still body of the priest, who was turned in his direction, his eyes open.

Sanchez rubbed his face and asked the priest what he was doing, staring at him like that, while he was asleep. Enough already, said Sanchez. You're creeping me out.

My arm hurts, said the priest.

Sanchez looked at his watch. It was time. He got up and put on his boots, jacket, and gloves. I'm going for a walk, he said.

There's something wrong with me, said the priest. I don't feel right.

You'll be okay. Just get some rest and take it easy. Sanchez looked at the priest and his face was frail, bloodless, almost a blue color. He closed his eyes and even his eyelids were wrinkled. What hope for an old timer such as he? What thought of second chance? A sad thing he was. An old man with a head full of sin memories and a chant of prayers to ward off the cold.

Outside the cabin, Sanchez zipped his parka, pulled on his knit cap, and headed downhill, toward the cemetery. The snow squeaked beneath his boots. He passed through the forest of ponderosa pines into which a curtain of powdery snow drifted down like flour from a sifter. He was alone in the woods and heard only the hoots of owls calling to each other high in the branches of the pines.

When he reached the cemetery he headed toward a Subaru parked outside the gates, exhaust coughing out its tailpipe. Behind the steering wheel sat his sister-in-law. After he climbed inside the car they kissed and held each other close, not saying a word. She was crying a little and he told her to stop it. Everything was going to be all right. He was getting better and he'd be out before she could say boo. She wiped away her tears and smiled, her lips trembling. Her hair was bleached blonde and wispy. Sanchez could see she had made herself up for him, could see she wore lip gloss and that her eyes were darkened with mascara and shadow. She said she didn't know if she could stand it, waiting for him to get out.

Sanchez touched her face, lifted her downcast chin. I'm here now, aren't I?

She nodded. You're here.

He smoothed a blonde strand of her hair behind her ear. Do you want to get into the back seat?

I don't know. Someone might be coming.

For what?

To pay their respects.

On a Tuesday? In the snow?

They got out of the car and shut the front doors, then opened the back doors and climbed into the back seat. They kissed for a moment. She tugged down her underthings. She pointed her toes and wriggled free from her shoes, and he worked the panties off her feet. She straddled his lap and then he was inside her. It was so wet and warm he was delirious. He felt as if he were melting. As if he could die a happy man. In this instant. He shivered and trembled and when it was over, he sat panting, jeans about his ankles. Blue shadows tinged the car's interior, the snow falling heavier, encasing the windows in a white cocoon.

Later he watched her car pull away, exhaust like a tail of smoke, her giving him one final, hopeful wave with her left hand before setting her face, unhappy as it would turn, on the way back to her husband and all things she would be. What they had just done now only a memory she would carry with her. He turned to the path out the back of the cemetery, uphill to the conference center, his rehab Sing Sing.

The pines held a fresh icing of snow and the flakes drifted like something pure and special. In that moment, with the smell of her still upon his hands and his lips, Sanchez felt good. He thought of nothing but the snow and the taste of her still on his lips and felt terrific. Soon he would be in the cabin he shared with the defrocked priest. Soon his life would resume its forlorn and inevitable course.

When Sanchez returned to the cabin he would find the ex-priest fallen upon the floor, his face twisted in a grimace, his forehead propped awkwardly on the floor heater vent, skin scorched purple from the heat. This he did not yet know. He trudged up the hill, thinking of nothing but the sweet, sad touch of this woman he was ill-fated to want, and the loveliness of the snow, and the sound of a horned owl hooting in the branches above.

# ACKNOWLEDGMENTS

The following stories originally appeared, in slightly different
form, in these journals:

| | |
|---|---|
| *Alaska Quarterly Review* | "Warsaw, 1984" |
| *Cutbank* | "The Next Worst Thing" |
| *Descant* | "What Happens to Rain?" |
| *Echo Ink Review* | "Playboys" |
| *Gulf Coast* | "This Whatever We Have" |
| *The Hopkins Review* | "The Hidden Jesus" |
| | "The Lousy Adult" |
| | "The Sea Horse" |
| *Press* | "That Night at the Café" |

## FICTION TITLES IN THE SERIES

Guy Davenport, *Da Vinci's Bicycle*

Stephen Dixon, *14 Stories*

Jack Matthews, *Dubious Persuasions*

Guy Davenport, *Tatlin!*

Joe Ashby Porter, *The Kentucky Stories*

Stephen Dixon, *Time to Go*

Jack Matthews, *Crazy Women*

Jean McGarry, *Airs of Providence*

Jack Matthews, *Ghostly Populations*

Jack Matthews, *Booking in the Heartland*

Jean McGarry, *The Very Rich Hours*

Steve Barthelme, *And He Tells the Little Horse the Whole Story*

Michael Martone, *Safety Patrol*

Jerry Klinkowitz, *Short Season and Other Stories*

James Boylan, *Remind Me to Murder You Later*

Frances Sherwood, *Everything You've Heard Is True*

Stephen Dixon, *All Gone: 18 Short Stories*

Jack Matthews, *Dirty Tricks*

Joe Ashby Porter, *Lithuania*

Robert Nichols, *In the Air*

Ellen Akins, *World Like a Knife*

Greg Johnson, *A Friendly Deceit*

Guy Davenport, *The Jules Verne Steam Balloon*

Guy Davenport, *Eclogues*

Jack Matthews, *Storyhood as We Know It and Other Tales*

Stephen Dixon, *Long Made Short*

Jean McGarry, *Home at Last*

Jerry Klinkowitz, *Basepaths*

Greg Johnson, *I Am Dangerous*

Josephine Jacobsen, *What Goes without Saying: Collected Stories*

Jean McGarry, *Gallagher's Travels*

Richard Burgin, *Fear of Blue Skies*

Avery Chenoweth, *Wingtips*

Judith Grossman, *How Aliens Think*

Glenn Blake, *Drowned Moon*

Robley Wilson, *The Book of Lost Fathers*

Richard Burgin, *The Spirit Returns*

Jean McGarry, *Dream Date*

Tristan Davies, *Cake*

Greg Johnson, *Last Encounter with the Enemy*

John T. Irwin and Jean McGarry, eds., *So the Story Goes: Twenty-five Years of the Johns Hopkins Short Fiction Series*

Richard Burgin, *The Conference on Beautiful Moments*

Max Apple, *The Jew of Home Depot and Other Stories*

Glenn Blake, *Return Fire*

Jean McGarry, *Ocean State*

Richard Burgin, *Shadow Traffic*

Robley Wilson, *Who Will Hear Your Secrets?*

William J. Cobb, *The Lousy Adult*